Remy and Rose'- A Hood Love Story

Mz.Lady P

Copyright 2014 2015 by Mz. Lady P

Published by Shan Presents

www.shanpresents.com

All rights reserved

This book is a work of fiction. Names, characters, places, and incidents either are the product of the author's imagination or are used fictitiously and are not to be construed as real. Any resemblance to actual persons, living or dead, business establishments, events, or locales or, is entirely coincidental.

No portion of this book may be used or reproduced in any manner whatsoever without writer permission except in the case of brief quotations embodied in critical articles and reviews.

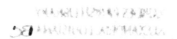

Text SHAN to 22828 to stay up to date with new releases, sneak peeks, contest, and more...

Table of Contents

Chapter 1- Rose' Richards

(Rozay)

Love has a way of making a person do some crazy ass shit. I'll be the first to admit that being in love with the wrong nigga has put me in a fucked up situation. I'm Rose' Richards and I'm twenty-one years old. I've just served four years of a five-year prison sentence for drug possession. As I sit on my bunk waiting to be released later on today, all I can do is think about my first love, Ace Black.

I was sixteen and he was twenty when I first met him. I would see him every day after school, hugging the block on the Westside of Chicago. He was fine as hell, rocked a low-cut fade, a little on the stocky side, and his attire stayed on point, despite the fact he was always loud and rambunctious. Ace was the nigga that your mother warned you not to fall in love with. I was no fool. I knew he was selling drugs, though I didn't really know anybody who did. I wasn't allowed to hang with those types of people.

My mother, Sherita, was the head nurse at Rush Presbyterian Hospital. She worked long hours and kept me on a tight leash. The only thing I was allowed to do was go to school and come straight home afterwards. On the weekends,

I was allowed to go over my father's house. My father, Dino, stayed in the heart of K-Town. That's where all the shit popped off at on the weekends, so I was more than happy to spend my weekends there.

My mother hated my father with a passion and I was always in the middle of their constant bickering, especially when it came down to the freedom I had at his house. I used to have so much fun over there with my cousins. They stayed on the same block with our grandmother who we called Madear. I was really close with my cousins Boo and Peanut. They were some wild ass niggas and forever stayed in trouble. I let them get me into all types of shit. I laughed to myself as I thought about the numerous punishments I got on fucking with them.

One day I was walking home from school and Ace approached me. He had on an all-white T-shirt with all black Levi's. He wore a pair of crispy white Air Force Ones. I was nervous as hell as he approached me. Females were always around him so I was curious as to why he was trying to holler at me.

"Slow down little momma. You walk past me every day and never even speak to a nigga. I'm truly hurt." He put his hand over his heart like he was really hurt.

"Boy please, you don't speak to me either." I had my hands on my hips as I spoke to him.

"Don't ever call a grown man a boy. That's disrespectful. You should come upstairs and chill with me for a minute," he whispered in my ear, causing me to get goose bumps all over my body.

"I don't know you like that."

"Quit playing Rose'. You know I'm cool with Boo and Peanut."

I couldn't believe he knew my name. I thought long and hard, before I gave in and went upstairs in the apartment building that he lived in. In situations like this, your mind is telling you don't go but your heart is like go with the flow. As we entered the house, I knew it had to be a female's apartment. It had a lady's touch to it.

"Come on. Let's go to the back in the room. I don't like to smoke in the living room; that smell gets in the furniture."

I should have walked my ass out the front door right then and there. Instead, I followed him in the room. We both sat on the bed and he fired up a blunt.

"So, tell me something about the beautiful Rose'."

"I mean, there's not much to tell. I'm sixteen, I go to Westinghouse Vocational High School, I'm a sophomore and I live out in Oak Park with my mother."

During our conversation, I learned his age and a little about his family. Not much else. It was like he really wasn't trying to go into detail about himself. His focus was more on the blunt he rolled. I really didn't smoke but I didn't want to seem like a lame, although my ass was. The only time I would ever hit a blunt was when I was with my cousins, but I went ahead and smoked the blunt with him.

"Has anyone ever told you how beautiful you are?"

Ace was rubbing all on my legs and the weed had me feeling all hot. I was a virgin, so I wasn't really sure why my coochie was dripping. I shook my head 'no' as he stood up in front of me. He pulled his shirt over his head and took off his pants. He was standing in front of me with dick standing at attention. I was eye level with his tool. I had to blink a couple of times to make sure I wasn't dreaming. I was just looking at him in awe. I started to get scared so I jumped up to leave because I wasn't ready to go here with him.

"You feel that shit." Ace had grabbed my hand and guided my hands up and down his shaft.

"Look Ace, I like you and all but I'm a virgin. I've never done this before," I spoke nervously, but I never stopped massaging his shaft. His eyes lit up when he heard me say I was a virgin. He had this devilish smirk on his face. I should have got my ass up and left.

"A virgin, huh?" He pushed me back on the bed and pulled my yoga pants down, got on his knees and started licking my pussy. I was trying my best to squirm out of his grasp, but he had a death grip on my legs. My body was shaking and twitching as a gush of fluid escaped me.

"What was that Ace? Did I just pee in your mouth?"

"No baby that was your sweet nectar. It tasted good too. Now lay back on the bed."

He laid on top of me and positioned himself in between my legs. I closed my eyes tight as he fought to get the head in.

"Please stop Ace, it hurts." I tried pushing him off of me. He pinned my arms behind my head and rammed his dick in me with so much force, that tears rolled down my face as he thrust in and out of me. It hurt like hell, but eventually it started to feel good.

"This my pussy now, Rose'. You better not give my shit to nobody."

He was still thrusting in and out of me, until finally his body started to shake on top of me. He stood up and walked to the bathroom to clean himself up. He then brought a towel and washed my pussy for me. His touch felt so good; but in my mind, I knew this shit was wrong.

"I don't want you to think I'm the type of nigga that will take your virginity and stop fucking with you. However, no one can know about this or about us. You're my woman now but because of our age difference, shit has to be on the low low. Remember what I said, that's my pussy now. So I better not hear about or even think you fucking with another nigga. Ya feel me beautiful?"

Ace was now tonguing me down. All I could do was agree with what he was saying. In a matter of hours, Ace had me eating out the palm of his hands. That was my first act of stupidity over Ace Black, but it definitely wasn't my last.

****

"I'm telling you Rose', we need to go to this block party," my best friend Diamond said, as she stood in front of her floor length mirror in her room, making sure her clothes were straight.

"I already told your ass I can't. Ace doesn't want me to go to the block party. Plus, I don't want to see Ace all in other bitches face." Once the words left my mouth, I knew Diamond was about to curse my ass out. She was very verbal and outspoken.

"You know you my bitch, but I wouldn't be a friend if I didn't keep it all the way one hundred with you. Ace don't give a fuck about you, Rose'. That nigga has so many bitches it's ridiculous. You are too smart of a girl to let him have mind control over you like this. Has it ever occurred to you that he's just using you for sex and to make drug runs for him?"

A month after we had sex I started doing drug runs with him on the weekends. My mother would kill me dead if she knew the shit I had been doing.

"Ace is not using me, Diamond. He loves me. It's just that he will get in trouble with the law if it were ever known that we fuck around."

"Whatever Rose'. Let yourself out, I'm about to go turn up. I'm too young and pretty to let a nigga dictate my pace."

I sat there and let it marinate. She was right. Ace fucked around all the time but I wasn't allowed to. I knew he was going to be mad at me when he saw me. He wouldn't go off in front of everybody, so I would just deal with that later.

"Fuck it, I'm going with you." I did a once over in the mirror and I was ready to go.

My long hair was pulled back in a ponytail. It was hot as hell outside, so I had on a low-cut top with a mini skirt on, and a pair of all white Puma's with no socks. Once we made it on Karlov, the block party was in full swing. The kids were all playing in the bouncy houses, the grills were going, and of course, all the niggas and females were posted all up and down the block, with their car systems going and drinks flowing.

"Come on bitch, there go Boo and Peanut right there." Diamond practically ran trying to get to Peanut. She was so in love with him, but he didn't pay her ass a lick of attention.

"What's up cuz?" I said to Boo and Peanut as we all hugged. Not long after, the rest of their crew joined us on the corner.

"Where the hell you going in this little ass skirt?" Mook said as he tugged it at the bottom.

I looked up and locked eyes with Ace. His jaws were clenched so tight, I knew he was going to act a fool. Mook really hadn't done anything. Plus, he was like family. I already knew Ace was going to assume I was fucking him.

For the rest of the day, I watched Ace entertain different females. He was being real disrespectful, but there was really nothing I could do since no one could know about us but us. He would have a fit if he knew Diamond knew about us. It was starting to get dark and I knew Ace wanted me to go home with him tonight. It was the weekend so my parents would think I was with Diamond.

"I'm about to head home. I'll see ya'll tomorrow." I started walking like I was going towards the bus stop to catch the Blue Line train home. I was really going to meet up with Ace so that we can go in the house together.

His Impala was parked on the corner when I made it there. He unlocked the passenger side door and I got in. I leaned over to kiss him but he punched me hard as hell in the mouth.

"Didn't I tell your ass not come to that party?"

I was in shock, as blood seeped through my fingers while I held my mouth. The blow was so painful that I couldn't speak. All I could do was nod my head yes. Next, I was met with a slap to the face that caused my head to bounce off of the passenger side window.

"Cat got your motherfucking tongue now? You was running off at the mouth with them niggas earlier. Open your mouth and say something before I slap the fuck outta your hoe ass again…out here in these streets acting like a hoe with these little ass clothes on."

"I'm sorry, Ace. I just wanted to come outside. Plus, you were in other females' faces the entire time I was there." I was crying and still holding my mouth because blood was leaking out like a faucet.

"Shut the fuck up with your young, dumb ass. So because you see me talking to bitches, you're going to turn around and talk to niggas in my face? What the fuck is this, monkey sees monkey motherfucking do?"

"You know Boo and Peanut are my cousins. Why are you doing this to me?"

"That nigga Mook put his hand up your skirt."

"No he didn't Ace."

"So, you're calling me a liar, Rose'?"

"No. I'm just saying that he didn't put his hands up my skirt. All he did was tug at the bottom of it." I was trying my best to plead my case but I had fucked up when I told him he even touched me at all. The slaps he was delivering to my face was coming in rapid succession. I could no longer block his hands, so I just sat there and let him smack me until he got tired. I was crying hard as hell.

"Wipe your motherfucking face and stop all that crying. You brought this shit on yourself. I'm sorry that I put my hands on you like this, but when I tell you to do something you do it. Go in the house and clean your face. I'm about to go get us some food so have my room cleaned when I get back."

He leaned over and kissed me and of course I kissed him back. I loved him and he had my mind so gone, I really felt that he only did what he did because he loved me. That was my second act of stupidity. But as the old saying goes, the third time is a charm.

9

A couple of months after that incident, things were going well between us. My mother was working more and more shifts, so she really had no idea what was going on with me. Each weekend I had been riding down to Fon Du Lac, Wisconsin, doing drug runs with Ace. I had just turned seventeen, so he was a little bit more comfortable with me riding with him.

On this particular trip, I had an eerie feeling about things. I just wanted to get things over with and make it back home. As soon as we got on the Bishop Ford Expressway, a police car pulled us over.

"Oh shit! Put all this in your purse and say that it's yours. I'm going to come and bond you out. You're underage so you won't get any time. I love you Rose'." Ace kissed me passionately and gave me the biggest hug ever.

"I love you too, Ace."

I put all the packaged drugs in my purse. When the officer arrived and he checked the car, they found the drugs in my purse. Of course my stupid in love ass took the weight. At the time I trusted Ace. I believed everything he said. It wasn't until I was standing in front of the judge being sentenced to five years, did I realize I had made the biggest mistake of my life.

My mother and father tried their best to get me out, but because I took ownership of the drugs, I was charged with 'Possession with the Intent to Distribute'. To make matters worse, two weeks after I was arrested, I found out I was almost three months pregnant with Ace's baby. My mother was livid, so she cut off all ties with me. To add insult to injury, I haven't seen or heard from Ace since the day I was arrested. No phone call, no letters, or visits. He doesn't even know we have a four-year-old daughter I named Heaven Acearia Black.

Once I gave birth, she was turned over to my father and he has been raising her ever since. If it wasn't for my father's side of the family, I don't think I would have made it out. I just want to start my life over and raise my daughter. I can't help but wonder how her father would feel knowing that she existed.

☐

Chapter 2- Meeting Remy

I was nervous the entire ride home on the Greyhound Bus. Four years felt like forty years to me. Jail had really put the pounds on my body, but in a good way. When I first came in, I was petite as hell. They always say the jail food is nasty, but that shit had me thicker than a snicker. Not to mention my cellie had created some type of hair mayonnaise that had my shit damn near to the middle of my back. Jail had done my body good, but fucked my mind up. Not that I was crazy or anything, but being confined to that small ass space did something to me.

As I walked down the block to my father's home, I could see so many people standing outside and cars lined up and down the block. I started crying when I saw my family holding 'Welcome Home' signs and balloons. I dropped to my knees when I saw Heaven dressed in her pretty pink tutu and blinged out Chuck Taylors. Her little shirt said "Welcome Home Mommy". She ran straight to me and I hugged her, crying my heart out. I picked her up and placed her on my hip.

"That's enough of that crying. Welcome home, baby. We missed you." My Daddy hugged and kissed me. Over the years we had become so close. He brought my baby to see me every month and that's what kept me going.

"Is my mother here?" I only asked because a part of me wished that she would have come. Of course that was wishful thinking.

"Hell no that she devil ain't here. She's not welcome here either," my Daddy said and I knew he meant every word.

The house was filled up with all of my family. Madear had cooked so much food; I couldn't wait to tear some shit up.

"Look who the fuck they let up out that jam," Peanut said, as him and Boo walked towards me with his their arms stretched out wide.

"I missed ya'll so much." I hugged both of them tightly. While I was in prison, they made sure to keep money on my books. Boo and Peanut were now heavy in the drug game and was getting major money.

"Come on everybody. Let's eat."

My grandmother started making every one a plate. I hurried up and ate two plates back to back. For the rest of the night we partied. Nothing had changed about Peanut and Boo. They were still the life of the party. Sadness took over me because I didn't have anything. I couldn't even buy my daughter a bag of chips from the store.

"What's up beautiful? I thought being released from prison was a good thing. You're over here looking all sad and shit. Wipe those tears, pretty lady," the deepest voice I've ever heard spoke, causing me to look up. I had no idea who this stranger was, but he must have been created by the Greek gods themselves. He was tall and looked like he was mixed with something, but he could pass as being fully black. His dreads were long as hell and braided down his back in a neat fishtail.

He was dressed in an all-black linen suit with some Salvatore Ferragamo loafers on his feet. His iced out pinky ring and Rolex watch was blinding me. He handed me a napkin and I wiped my tears away with it. I was immediately embarrassed as I looked down at my jail house attire. I never got a chance to change when I first arrived.

"Thank you for the napkin. I'm Rose' by the way."

"Nice to meet you, I'm Remy." I extended my hand to shake his, but instead, he pulled me in close and gave me a hug. His Tom Ford cologne invaded my nostrils.

"So tell me why you're over here crying when you have a thousand reasons to smile?"

"I don't know what the future holds for me and my daughter. I'm just trying to figure out what I'm going to do now that I'm out. I just made twenty-one and I have no job experience. I received my G.E.D while I was locked up, but that will only take me so far. The shit is just frustrating to me."

"I know you don't know me but I own several businesses. How about you come to my strip club tomorrow at three? I've been looking for a new bartender, and you're beautiful. With a little training I know you will get the hang of it. Actually, I'm not accepting no for an answer, so I'll see you tomorrow at three. Here's my business card and some money for clothes. Dress to impress; first impressions are everything."

He walked away from me like it was nothing. I still had my mouth open at his straight forwardness. I guess that's what a 'boss' is. He just bossed the fuck up on my ass.

"Close your mouth before something flies in it," Boo said as he came and sat next to me.

"Do you know that guy over there in all black?"

"Yeah, that's my big homie Remy."

"He just offered me a job and basically told me I couldn't refuse."

"Remy is the man, cuz. No one tells him no. Make sure you be on point for the interview. He doesn't like it when you're late." He kissed me on the forehead and went over and stood alongside Remy and Peanut.

Boo thinks he's slick. He probably set all that shit up. Later that night, I lay on the floor in my daughter's room and stared at the card. I was so nervous about the next day I couldn't sleep; instead, I sat up and watched my daughter as she slept. It was crazy how she looked nothing like me. She was her father's twin. I hated that she was in this fucked up situation because of my stupidity. I'm going to die trying to give her a better life.

****

The next morning I got up and went to Charlotte Rousse to find me something to wear to the interview. I settled on a pencil skirt and a nice blouse to match. I found a nice pair of heels that were high as hell. I wanted to look cute for Remy for some reason. I flat ironed my hair bone straight and put on a small coating of lip gloss. All this shit was so foreign to me after being locked up for so long. I was lost on what was in style. I just hoped he didn't look at my ass and laugh.

"Stop being so damn nervous cuz. You're going to do just fine," Peanut said as he drove me to the club.

"Have you seen Ace?"

"Fuck that nigga Rose'! He a bitch for making you take that weight for his ass. Me and Boo whooped dude's ass when we found out what the fuck went down. We've been beefing ever since. I'm telling you now, stay the fuck away from dude. He's grimy as fuck. I'll body that nigga on sight. You and Heaven ain't got shit to worry about, I got ya'll."

"I just asked because I wanted to let him know about Heaven. He has no idea that she exists."

"I understand all that cuz. I just don't want you getting all caught up in his madness. Plus, there's something you should know. He's married to Diamond and they have two kids."

"My friend Diamond?" He nodded his head in confirmation and I was in shock; mainly, because she always acted as if she hated Ace. I guess that explains why I never heard from her either.

"Fuck them cuz. Move on with your life. I know you want Ace to be in Heaven's life but he doesn't even deserve to know her." I couldn't even argue with Peanut. He was absolutely right. Ace wasn't worthy of knowing my daughter.

I made it to Club Kitty Kat about thirty minutes early. I walked in and there were some dancers performing on stage. I couldn't believe it was packed in here this damn early.

"Excuse me, I have an interview with Mr. Ramirez," I said to one of the bouncers. He spoke into his mouth piece and I was led to a set of elevators. I rode the elevator up to the second level. When the doors opened, Remy was standing there waiting for me.

"You clean up nice, beautiful. Follow me into my office."

Remy was dressed in jeans and a T-shirt with a pair of wheat Timberlands. His dreads were now hanging and they were down to the middle of his back. He went from straitlaced to thuggish, and he looked good as hell both ways.

"Thank you. I hope it's not too much."

"No, you're perfect. Here is your uniform and your gym shoes. I don't allow the bartenders to wear heels. I like for my girls to be comfortable. Is that okay with you? If the dress is too short for you, I'll have the seamstress get you a bigger size. Go in the bathroom and change so I can see you in your uniform.

"So I don't need to be interviewed?"

"You had the job the moment I laid eyes on you. Your pay is twenty dollars an hour and you keep all your tips. Payday is every other Friday. Is that okay with you, beautiful?"

"Yeah, that's okay. Thank you so much, Remy. I appreciate it."

I got up and fell dead on my ass. I was embarrassed as hell. I looked up and he was laughing so damn hard.

"Are you cool?" he asked as he lifted me up off of the floor.

"I'm just happy, that's all." I managed to laugh as well.

"I'm glad I can put a smile on your face. Now go get dressed. You start training at five."

I was staring in his eyes and they were the prettiest shade of brown. I was staring at him so hard I didn't realize I was still holding his hand. I hurried up and let it go and went to change.   Once I tried on the outfit, I was in shock at how my ass and titties had developed over the years. It was an all-black mini dress that had 'The Kitty Kat' on the front in pink letters. The all-white Air Force Ones also fit perfectly. It was like he knew what size I wore already.

"How do I look, boss man?" Remy was on the phone when I came back in his office. He hung up and walked around to where I was at.

"Damn beautiful. You look good in whatever you put on."

He took my hand and twirled me around in front of him so that he could take a good look at me. Remy had me feeling like a school girl. No man had ever complimented me so much or made me feel so special. I felt tingly every time he touched me. I couldn't get ahead of myself though. I was scared of the unknown. All I knew was Ace and he had me scared to give my heart again. Plus, the man before me was my boss.

For the rest of the night I trained, and it was fairly easy. I caught on quick as hell. There was another bartender by the name of Neicee and she was cool as hell. I later found out she messed around with my cousin Peanut. It was now one in the morning and the club was packed. There was a table requesting bottle service, so I had to take them the bottles they had requested. At first I was scared of them damn sparkles, but I eventually got use to them.

"Here go your bottles, gentlemen," I said, as I sat the bucket on the table along with their glasses.

"Damn baby. You're fine as fuck."

The voice immediately made me look up. It was Ace Black in the flesh and he was sexier than I remembered. We locked eyes and that's when he noticed me. I took off running towards the ladies' bathroom. I was crying and shaking so bad in front of the vanity. Seeing him so happy and living it up hurt me like a motherfucker.

After about five minutes, I gathered up the strength to get back to work. When I walked pass the table, Ace was gone. The rest of the night was a blur. I couldn't wait to get off and get home to my daughter. Once the club was over, I stood outside and waited for my cab. I shitted bricks when I saw Ace sitting outside in a cocaine white Benz.

Chapter 3- Ace

It had been so long since I thought about Rose'. I had no idea that she was even out of prison. I thought she was sentenced to five years. From time to time I would look her up in the Department of Corrections Inmate Search System. I felt bad how shit ended for her. I hated that I had to leave her hanging like that.

At the time I wasn't trying to be involved in any investigations. I had mad respect for her for taking that weight and never ratting me out. I sit back and think to when she was younger and how I had her wrapped around my finger. She would do any motherfucking thing I said, unlike the bitch Diamond who always has something to say. I know that Rose' was probably hurt when she found out that I married her friend. Unbeknownst to her, we had been fucking the entire time that I was dealing with her.

Rose' was real naive to obvious shit going on in her face, but I loved her beauty and her innocence. Seeing her tonight had me all in my feelings. She was even more beautiful and her body was banging. I got a hard on knowing that I hit that shit first. I wondered if she was fucking some chump ass nigga. I hope she wasn't because I had plans to get her back on my team. I didn't give a fuck about being married to

Diamond. Plus, Rose' shouldn't care about being my little secret, especially since that's what she was back in the day.

I sat outside my car and waited for her to get off work. As soon as she walked out she saw me, and was looking like a deer in head lights.

"Let me drop you off Rose'. It's too late for you to be out here."

"I'm good. My cab should be pulling up in a minute."

"Come on Rose'. I just want to talk to you for a minute." I could tell she was about to make this shit hard for me.

"We don't have anything to talk about, Ace. I actually have no words for you. Leave me alone. I lost four years out of my life and you moved on with yours. It's water under the bridge. Do us both a favor and go home to your family." She tried walking past, but I grabbed her by her wrists.

"Don't forget who the fuck you talking to Rose'."

"Get your fucking hands off of me."

"Do we have a problem here?" Remy said as he walked up with his gun out.

"This shit don't concern you my nigga." I pulled my gun from my waist as well. I had been beefing hard with him and his crew over territory.

"Actually it has everything to do with me nigga. You're in front of my establishment harassing one of my employees. Go inside the club Rose'." This nigga Remy really thought he was running shit. Rose' yanked away from my grasp and hurriedly walked back inside.

"This shit ain't over Rose'. I'll see you around my nigga," I said as I backed away and went back to my car.

"You can see me now, bitch ass nigga!" Remy said as I drove away. It was imperative I off this nigga. It's bad enough he trying to take my traps from me, now he wants the one thing that belonged to me. Yeah, I need to get up with my niggas and put my plan in to motion. Since Rose' wanted to side with that nigga, I had something for her ass too. I know her best kept secret. She got me fucked up.

Chapter 4- Remy Ramirez

When I look back on my life, I can't help but feel blessed. In all of my twenty-six years, I've never had to struggle. I was born to the best parents a nigga could ever ask for. I wanted for nothing and never had to ask for anything.

As a young child, I knew that my family was different from others. Our house was always heavily guarded with security and outsiders were never allowed into our home. I wasn't even allowed to go to public school. My father, Reco, was a businessman, but he was never too busy to spend time with his one and only son. It was him who taught me how to do business and take a motherfucker out if I had to.

My mother, Mariah, hated that my father was grooming me to be the next in line to take over his spot in the family business. As a kid, I didn't know that one day I would be head of the Mexican Cartel. My father is of Mexican decent and my mother is a beautiful African American woman who takes pride in her color. My father worshipped the ground my mother walks on and to this day, he still does. Despite being of different races, no one dared to ever speak or question him about loving a black woman.

Recently my father was diagnosed with Pancreatic Cancer. He called me down to Mexico for a meeting and turned the business over to me. It's been on and popping ever since. That's what I do behind the scenes. No one even knows who I really am and I want to keep it that way.   Peanut and Boo handle all the street shit while I run shit from several of my businesses. Don't get it twisted though. When it's time for me bust my guns, my shit blows in all directions and I never miss my target. I like to remain laid back and out of the scene. The less these niggas in the Chi know about me, the better.

Sometimes I sit back and think about how successful I am, with no real woman to share it with. Don't get me wrong, I can be with any bitch I choose, but a down ass bitch is hard to find. I can fuck a different bitch every day of the week if I want. I don't trust or loves these hoes though. In my position, you have to watch these bitches.

I know what type of woman a female is the first time we meet. It's crazy how women get excited over what a nigga is wearing or what type of car he's driving. All these hoes see is dollar signs when they see me. I don't mind taking care of a woman but there's levels to this shit. I'll spoil my woman rotten, but she has to have the same drive as me.

I need a woman who wants to better herself and at the same time, make me a better man. If you don't have any drive then your ass gets no conversation. End of discussion. I'm not a cocky nigga. I'm very humble. I just know what I want and what I like.

****

I wanted to blow this nigga's Ace, fucking brains out. He's been trying me for a minute now. I think it's time I give Peanut and Boo the go ahead to murder that nigga. That nigga had a lot of nerve even stepping to Rose' after he left her ass high and dry. What real nigga allows his bitch to do a bid for him?

I already knew the whole story about how she ended up in jail, and my heart went out to her. Not to mention I have a weak spot for a beautiful woman with a banging ass body and ambition. It amazed me how she was just released from prison and all she was worried about was how she was going to take care of her daughter. She didn't give a fuck about being free. I never even saw her take a drink or smoke a blunt at her coming home party.

Once we started to talk, I knew that I was going to give her a job. One thing about Rose' that stood out to me was that she was innocent, almost childlike. She deserved to be happy and Ace's ass was trying to fuck that up. He had another thing coming though. As long as I was alive and breathing, he would not ruin her life any more than he already had.

I walked back into the club to check on Rose' and she was sitting at the bar with her head down.

"Are you okay?" I asked her as I stroked her long ponytail.

"I'm sorry to bring this drama to your place of business. I understand if you have to let me go," she said with

29

tears streaming from her eyes. I've seen this girl cry more than I've seen her smile.

"I'm not firing you, Rose'. You haven't done anything to be fired."

I walked towards and wiped her tears from her eyes. I tried to get her to look in my face but I could tell she was either embarrassed or very shy.

"I'm up here, ma. Always make eye contact when you talk to someone," I said, as I grabbed her face and looked into her beautiful hazel eyes. She looked at me and I was lost in her eyes for a minute. I almost leaned in to kiss her pretty, pink lips. The sound of a car honking outside broke both of our trances.

"That must be my cab. Thanks for everything boss man. I really appreciate it."

She kissed me on the jaw and raced out of the club. I turned and watch as her ass jiggled like Jell-O as she ran away. I had to pour me a shot of Hennessy. It had been a minute since I was attracted to a woman like I am to Rose'. I had to shake it off though. She had a lot going on with her and I didn't want to add to that.

I hated that I never asked her about the Ace situation. If she wanted to talk about it, she would when she was ready. In the meantime, I would just make sure I kept eyes on that nigga. I had a funny feeling he was about to pull a stunt.

Chapter 5- Rose'

The next couple of weeks of working at the club were great. I had made over six thousand dollars and I was able to pay a security deposit and first month's rent for my new apartment. My father didn't want me or Heaven to move out, but we had to. He had put his life on hold to raise her while I was locked up. It was time for him to get his groove back.

I hadn't seen Ace since that night when I first saw him. I was still on edge because I knew he was somewhere lurking. Today was my off day, so I took Heaven to Chuck E. Cheese. She was having a ball and I was getting tired. It was time to go and she did not want to get out of the balls.

"Come on Heaven, baby. It's time to go." I looked but she was no longer in the balls. I started panicking immediately.

"Heaven! Heaven! Where are you?" I was running around and looking all over for her.

"I'm right here, Mommy."

I turned around and I almost shitted on the floor. Ace was bending down tying her shoes.

"Get over here right now, Heaven!"

Ace had a smirk on his face as he grabbed her hand and walked towards me. He got real close to me and showed me his gun.

"Turn around and walk your ass out of here. Don't try no bullshit or I'm going to take her and you will never see her again. After all, she is my seed right?"

I turned around and walked towards the exit, and he was right behind me pressing the gun in my back. I got in the front seat of his car and he strapped Heaven in the back. He got in and drove away at top speed.

"Why didn't you tell me I had a daughter?"

I was getting ready to respond but he backhanded me across the face.

"Don't even say shit. All this time you had a baby by me and I didn't know shit about it."

"Maybe if your bitch ass would have written or visited me in jail, you would have known. This shit is your fault, not mine. Let me and my daughter out of this fucking car." I started hitting the passenger side door. I kicked the dashboard so hard that I made it shift.

"You can stop all that bullshit before you upset my daughter. The only way I'm letting you out this car is if you're dead when I push your ass out. So shut the fuck up and enjoy the ride."

Tears streamed down my face because I was so scared for me and Heaven. Ace was crazy as hell back in the day, but he was a fucking psycho now. About an hour later, we pulled into an apartment complex on the Southside of Chicago. Heaven had fallen asleep. I tried to grab her, but he pushed me hard as hell.

"Get the fuck back. I got her."

He grabbed my arm and led me into the building. We walked up the stairs to the third floor, where he opened the door with a key and we went in. I stood by the door as he laid Heaven on the Chenille fabric sectional. He made sure to cover her up in a blanket.

"Bring your ass in the room."

He yanked me by my ponytail and walked me to the back, still holding my hair. In the other hand he still had the gun. I couldn't run or scream if I wanted to.

"Take all your motherfucking clothes off!"

"Why are you doing this to me, Ace? What have I ever done to you?"

He cocked back the gun and didn't respond. I immediately started stripping out of fear that he would pull the trigger. He stood up and started taking off his clothes.

"Please Ace! I can't do this with you."

"I already know you giving that nigga Remy my pussy. That's why I'm about to rip you a new asshole."

He grabbed me by my throat and pushed me down on the bed. I was now lying on my stomach. He wrapped my ponytail around his hands and yanked my head back so hard I thought he had given me whiplash. He forced his tongue in my mouth and I bit that motherfucker. I could taste his blood in my mouth. At this point, he rammed his dick in my virgin asshole and began to thrust in and out of me.

"Ahhh!" I screamed out in pain and tried to get away, but he was holding on to me for dear life.

"Stupid bitch." He hit me in the back of the head with the gun. The pain from being raped and from being hit with the gun caused me to pass out.

The next morning I woke up, still in the same room from the previous night. I tried to move but I was in too much pain. After a couple of minutes of struggling, I was finally able to stand. Blood was everywhere; all over my lower body and all in the bed. I knew he had ripped my ass for real.

I had to get out of this fucking apartment. My thoughts drifted to Heaven and I slowly made my way to the living room where he had put her on the couch. I hoped and prayed she was there but she wasn't and my heart dropped. I found a letter on the table that he wrote.

"Heaven is going to stay with me from now on. She's cool. I just want to get to know my daughter better."

I let out a blood curdling scream. Ace had kidnapped my baby. I fell to the floor and laid there until I got myself together. I had no way of calling anybody. I left my phone and purse back at Chuck E. Cheese.

I got inside the tub and rinsed all the blood off of me. My tears mixed with the blood as it went down the drain. After a while, I got out, put my clothes back on and got the fuck out of the apartment, but I made sure to take that letter with me.

As I walked I thought about Peanut and Boo. They were out of town on a business run for Remy. There was no way I could call my father and tell him Ace took Heaven. There was only one person I could tell and that was Remy.

I hailed a cab and made my way to the club. Thank God I had a twenty in my pants pocket. I paid him and went inside to the usual scene. Not making eye contact with anyone, I hopped on the elevator and rode it up to Remy's office. I didn't even think to knock; I just twisted the knob and rushed in. My eyes bulged out of my head, as I watched a chick on her knees, sucking Remy's big ass dick.

"Oh my God! I'm so sorry!" My hands covered my mouth as Remy pushed the girl off of him. He tried pulling up his pants and boxers, but they kept falling. His dick was huge and for some reason, I couldn't take my eyes off it. I rushed out of his office and ran downstairs to the employee bathroom, where I locked myself inside.

Seeing him with another girl made me sad, mainly because I had the biggest crush on him. Of course he didn't know that. Those emotions mixed with being raped and my daughter kidnapped had me fucked all the way up. I just sat on the floor and cried. Not long after, Remy was banging on the other side of the door for me to let him in.

Chapter 6- Remy

I was struggling like a motherfucker trying to put my dick up. It wasn't that I got caught up or anything, it's just that I didn't want her to see no shit like that. I saw that she was crying when she rushed out of my office. I had to find her and apologize. Rose' had told the other bartender, Neicee, that she was attracted to me. Of course Neicee's ass ran her mouth, trying to hook us up on the low. So I know her seeing me get some sloppy toppy from one of my randoms had her feeling some type of way.

"Open the door Rose'. Just come and talk to me. I'm sorry you had to see that shit." I was banging on the door, getting ready to kick the bitch in but she opened it. I put my head down as I noticed that her face was stained with tears. She fell in my arms and I hugged her tight.

"Ace raped me and he kidnapped Heaven. What am I going to do Remy?"

She was crying so bad that I had to lift her up because her legs had given out on her.

"Shhh! We're going to get her back, okay? I promise. I kissed her on the forehead, carried her out of the back door and put her inside my all black Lamborghini. I did the speed limit getting her to my crib.

"What the hell were you doing with that nigga?"

"I took Heaven to Chuck E. Cheese. He popped up out of nowhere and forced me and Heaven out of the place. We got in his car and he took us to some apartment. Heaven had fallen asleep so he laid her on the couch and forced me to the back bedroom. He made me strip and he-- he…"

I could tell she was embarrassed to tell the rest of the details. I swear I was going to murder this nigga with my bare hands.

"Shouldn't we call the police so that they can do an Amber Alert?"

"We can't call the police, Rose'. You already know he's a dead man. If we bring in the police and he turns up dead, we'll all be sitting in prison. Look at me Rose'. Do you trust that I will protect you and get Heaven back?"

"Yes. I trust you Remy."

I could tell she was unsure, but I would just have to make her a believer. We pulled up to my home in Country Club Hills. I carried her into the house and upstairs to one of the guest bedrooms. I sat her down on the bed, went inside the bathroom and ran her some bathwater. When I came out, she was just sitting there in a daze.

"Rose', I need to get you cleaned up. Is it okay if I undress you?" She nodded her head 'yes' so I slowly removed her shirt. I hoped and prayed my dick behaved because this was the wrong time to be getting erect. I stood her up and removed her pants. I cringed because there was so much blood on her pants.

"I think I should take you to the hospital."

"No Remy. I don't want them to ask all those questions. It's too embarrassing."

"I understand you're embarrassed. However, you have no reason to be. I think you might need some stitches in your vaginal area."

"That's not where I need them at."

She got up and slowly walked inside the bathroom, closing the door behind her. I sat on the edge of the bed with my head down in my hands. I needed a drink because this shit was too much. I went into my office and grabbed a fifth of Hennessy and drunk straight from the bottle, then hit Boo and Peanut and let them know they needed to get back here ASAP. I also hit up her Pops and let him know what was going on. Dino was an OG so he knew no police could be called. He ran all my chicken shacks I had across the city. Rose' didn't have to know that though. After knocking back a couple more shots, I went to check on Rose'.

I stepped inside the room and she was standing in front of the floor length mirror, naked. It looked like she was trying to look and see behind her. I tried to hurry up and turn around but she had already seen me.

"I need you to look back there Remy."

"Back where?" I looked at her ass like she was crazy.

"I want you to see if there's a tear or something. I'm still bleeding really badly. I trust you Remy. Please do it. I don't want to go to the hospital and let a stranger do it."

Rose' didn't even give me a chance to say no. She laid flat on her stomach. From where I was standing, I could see handprints and bruising all over her ass. That shit made me mad. I was ready to explode.

I really didn't want to check her; that was some shit a doctor should be doing. Nevertheless, I sat on the side of the bed and put my hands or her cheeks.

"Let me know if I'm hurting you," I said as I gently pulled her ass cheeks apart to see. There was a little bit of tearing. The blood wasn't coming out as much as she thought it was. I don't know why I did it, but I leaned down and placed soft kisses on both of her ass cheeks. She jumped a little from the touch of my lips.

"I'm sorry. I just wanted to kiss it and make you feel better. There's a little tearing and you're not bleeding a lot. I think you need to just soak in hot water a couple of times a day. There are some shirts in the dresser; fell free to put one on. I'm going to lie down, and tomorrow we're going to get Heaven."

"Please don't leave me by myself, Remy." She jumped up and ran into my arms.

"Come on, you can sleep in my room." I watched as she grabbed a t-shirt and a pair of boxers and put them on. We both walked into my bedroom and laid in bed. Since I didn't feel comfortable sleeping naked, I made sure I was fully clothed. I wanted her to feel as comfortable as possible.

"Thanks for making me feel better," Rose' said as she kissed me on my lips. That shit caught me by surprise like a motherfucker. Something was going to have to give real soon. Rose' had me feeling some type of way.

****

The next morning I woke up and Rose' was sleeping peacefully next to me. She was beautiful even with drool seeping out the corner of her mouth. I looked over and checked my phone for any missed calls and noticed a couple from both Boo and Peanut, telling me their plane had landed and they would be here shortly. I got up and decided to cook breakfast. I looked in the fridge and there wasn't shit to cook. Since Rose' was sleeping so good, I dipped out and grabbed breakfast from McDonalds. I was gone for like thirty minutes. When I came back to check on Rose', she was sitting up in bed with her legs pulled up to her chest. I could tell that she had been crying.

"Are you hungry, ma?"

"I don't have an appetite. I just want my baby back."

"Do you think Ace will hurt her?"

"No. He was so sweet to her. I think he took her to teach me a lesson. Knowing Ace, he has my daughter at the crib with him and Diamond."

"What do you mean teach you a lesson?"

"Before I got locked up, if I did anything he didn't like he would beat me up. He always said he was just teaching me a lesson. I think his attack on me the other night was about you. He thinks we're messing around. He hated that I walked away from him that night of the incident outside of the club. He takes pride in knowing that he had me first. It's driving him crazy just thinking I gave away what he thinks belongs to him."

"Do you belong to him?" I was curious to know, because after all that she has been through for this nigga, she still seems weak-minded for his ass.

"No I don't belong to him. I regret the day I let him get in my head. He ruined my life back then and he's ruining my life right now. I'm never going to be happy as long as he's alive. Believe me when I tell you Remy, that part of my life is over. I just want to raise my daughter and know what it's like to have someone love me for me. I never want to experience this much pain from another man in my life. I know Ace though, and he'll never let me be happy; even though he's married to my ex friend Diamond. He thought I belonged to him then and he thinks I belong to him now."

"Know that I got you. That nigga will get what's coming to him. I'll take care of you and Heaven the rest of ya'll lives if I have to. That's my word."

"Why are you so nice to me?"

"Because you deserve to be happy." My phone started to ring and I answered. It was Neicee letting me know that we needed to get down to the club immediately.

"Get dressed; we need to get to the club." I waited for her to get dressed and about twenty minutes later, we were at the club. Boo and Peanut pulled up at the same time we did. We went inside and Heaven was sitting on top of the bar eating popcorn.

"Heaven baby, are you okay?" Rose' rushed over to Heaven and checked her out to see if she was okay. She kissed and hugged her so tight.

"How did you get Heaven?" I asked Neicee.

"When I came in to do inventory, she was sitting outside on the steps all by herself. I wish I knew who the fuck left her here all alone. I would fuck their asses up." Neicee was just as upset as the rest of us were.

"I swear to God, Ace is a dead ass nigga when I see him," Boo said as he paced back and forth.

"Who brought you here, Heaven?" Rose' asked.

"Ms. Diamond did. My Daddy told her to keep an eye on me until he came back, but she got mad because I cried for my Daddy. When he left she spanked me because I wouldn't stop crying, and that's when she left me by myself. I had fun with my Daddy but Ms. Diamond was mean."

Although Ace was going to get what was coming to him, it was good to know that he didn't mistreat his daughter. I looked at Rose' and I could tell she was happy he hadn't hurt her either.

"Take Rose' and Heaven back to my crib. Call me as soon as y'all get there, and make sure to stay there until I arrive." I handed my keys to Neicee as Rose' looked at me with a scared look on her face. I gave her a nod of assurance, letting her know that everything would be okay and I was right behind her. Boo and Peanut hugged and kissed her and Heaven. Once the girls were gone, we got right down to the business at hand.

"So what's the plan, boss? I'm ready to off this nigga. We can't let him keep walking around, letting him breathe while he's making my cousin's life miserable," Peanut said as he fired up a blunt.

"That nigga has to go," Boo added.

"I totally agree. Ya'll know we have to do this shit right. Rose' is our main concern right now but this shit is about territory as well. I want ya'll to burn all his traps to the ground. I don't want him to make another dime. I want somebody on him at all times. If that nigga taking a shit, some motherfucking body better be there to smell it. I'm going to keep Rose' and Heaven at my house. I think that's the safest place for her now. Ya'll already know I got her. I just want ya'll to handle this business accordingly with no fuck ups.

"We got you, boss. Aye, don't be over there falling all in love with my cousin and shit," Boo said and we all laughed.

They knew that I had a little thing for Rose' but I wouldn't act on it until I knew that she was ready for all of that. Truth be told, I really wouldn't act on it until I knew I was ready. We sat around and chopped it up until I left to check on Rose' and Heaven.

****

When I walked into the house, Neicee was sitting on the couch watching TV. I went and sat next to her and leaned my head back. When I looked over at her, she was smiling at me, looking crazy.

"What the hell you looking at, Neicee?"

"I'm looking at you. You like her don't you?"

"Like who? What the hell are you talking about?" I knew exactly who and what she was talking about, I just wanted to fuck with her for a minute.

"Don't play Remy. You have a thing for Rose' and I know for a fact she's feeling you. Ya'll need to cut the shit and take it to the next level. Big bro, that girl needs a man like you. The way you cater to her is amazing."

"What do you mean amazing? I'm just looking out for her."

"Must I paint a picture for you, nigga? Rose' has been through some shit and right now you're her knight in shining armor. You're the type of man most women dream of. Men like you come once in a lifetime. You have all this success and no one to share it with. Right now you have a single beautiful woman lying in your bed. Stop playing and wife her. Ace might be the only nigga she's been with sexually, but you're the only man that has captured her heart. Now let that marinate. Anyways, let me get the hell out of here. I have a date with my baby." Neicee has always been the voice of reason with her nosey ass. I can tell her and Rose' have been talking about me.

"Thanks Niecee. Tell that nigga Peanut he better not get lost in the pussy and forget he has a job to do."

"I got you, boss. Don't forget what I told you."

Neicee walked out of the door and I laid my head back on the couch in deep thought about the shit she said. Was I really ready for a committed relationship and fatherhood? Being with Rose' would mean I would become a permanent fixture in Heaven's life, not that it's an issue. I just don't know what the hell to do. I'm thinking way head of myself.

The sound of my phone vibrating brought me out of my thoughts. Looking at the screen I quickly answered. It was my mother calling long distance from Mexico. Nothing could prepare me for the news she had just given me. My father had just lost his battle with cancer. I needed to be on a plane immediately; my mother needed me right now.

Chapter 7- Rose'

I felt like I was floating on clouds as I lay in Remy's bed. His Givenchy cologne was all over his sheets and bedspread. The mere sight of him makes me blush. I have to close my legs tight each and every time his soft hands touch my skin. When he kissed my ass cheeks, I almost moaned out in pleasure. His lips felt like magic and I really did start to feel better, despite Ace assaulting me.

My pussy was craving for something I hadn't had in years. That was sex. I wanted Remy to make love to me and teach me how to please him. I wished I had the courage to tell him how I feel but I just don't. I know that everything he's doing for me is because he's a good person. The last thing I would want to do is ruin our friendship.

I was so glad Heaven had finally gone to sleep. All she did was talk about Ace. He must have really showed her a good time because she was smitten with him. I wasn't quite sure how I felt about that. I want her in his life, but I want him to stay the fuck away from me. I was no match for Ace, but I hoped Boo and Peanut make that nigga suffer when they get a hold of his ass. Me on the other hand, I couldn't wait to see that bitch Diamond. She had an ass whooping with her name written all over it.

I was thirsty so I got up to go get me a bottle of water. I walked pass the living room and Remy was sitting on the couch, with his head down in his hands. I walked around the couch and stood in front of him and I heard him sniffling like he was crying.

"What's wrong Remy?"

He pulled me close to him and wrapped his arms around my waist. He laid his head on my stomach and cried like a baby. I rubbed my hands through his dreads trying to comfort him.

"He's gone, ma."

"Who's gone?"

"My father died. I can't believe this shit. My father is my hero."

"Don't cry. He wouldn't want you to be sad like this. I promise everything will be okay. I'm here for you just like you've been here for me. Please stop crying. You're going to make me cry and I know you're tired of me crying."

He laughed a little when I said that. He looked up at me and I wiped the tears from his eyes. He stood up and pulled me close to him. We stared in each other's eyes and I was lost in his. I don't know what came over me. I got on my tip toes and kissed him on his lips. I was surprised when he grabbed the back of my head and slipped his tongue in my mouth. His juicy lips and his tongue tasted so good. We kissed for several seconds before he broke it.

"I want you and Heaven to come to Mexico with me. I need you there with me. I can't do this by myself.

"Of course I'll go with you. I just need to go home and pack some things for us."

"Don't worry about that. We'll go to the mall before we hop on the plane. I need you to pack me some things and I need to make some phone calls before we head out."

He kissed me on the forehead and walked away towards his home office. I went to his room and started packing the things I thought he would need, no questions asked.

****

The plane ride to Mexico was long as hell. The entire ride I was so nervous. I didn't really think about it before I agreed to go. I was scared of how his family would look at me. He assured me his mother was a really nice woman and I had nothing to worry about. My family was so happy. They thought that we made such a good couple. That was crazy because we never put a label on anything that we were doing. All we did was kiss that one time and that was it. I really didn't know what we were doing, but I would wait for him to put a label on it. I don't want to get ahead of myself.

I looked over and he and Heaven were fast asleep. I was too nervous to sleep so I just read some books on the Kindle Fire that Remy bought me while we shopped.

Once we made it to Mexico, we had to get on a boat to get to his family's home. When I laid eyes on it, I was in awe because they basically lived on their own little island. It was gorgeous. It looked like something off of the old TV show *Lifestyles of the Rich and Famous*. There were huge statues at the front entrance of their estate; one of his parents and one of him. Everything looked like it was made of porcelain. It was hard to believe that he had all this luxury here, but he would rather live in Chicago.

"Mommy, it's so big," Heaven said as she ran around the yard.

"Yes it is, now come over here. Don't play on the nice grass." Everything was so immaculate. The last thing I needed was for her to be running all around like that.

"It's fine Rose'. Let her play. It's just grass, ma."

Remy grabbed my hand and we walked into his parent's home. We were greeted by his mother as soon as we made it through the entrance.

"I'm so glad you're finally here, son. I missed you so much."

His mother was hugging him and crying. I let his hand go and stepped back so they could have a moment. She was a nice looking older black woman. She had on an all-black pantsuit with huge diamonds on all of her fingers. Her hair was pulled back into a neat ponytail. Remy looked a lot like his mother.

"I would like for you to meet my friend Rose', and this is her daughter Heaven." Well he had just put a label on what we were: friends.

"Hello Mrs. Ramirez, nice to meet you. I'm so sorry for your loss."

I held my hand out, but she totally dismissed it. She looked at me and then down at my daughter. A look of contempt was on her face. I knew for a fact Remy saw how would rude she was being to me. He looked over that and it really made me mad, but I know that they're grieving right now.

"Magdalena, could you please take them out to the guest house and get them situated?" Remy said to who I suppose was the maid. She ushered us out of the door and to the guest house. The guest house was beautiful as hell. All black marble floors and high ceilings. There were murals of Remy painted on the walls. Once we were settled in, Magdalena left. I started unpacking our clothes and putting them away, then I bathed Heaven and put her to bed because it was already ten at night and it was way past her bedtime.

Once she was asleep, I decided to open a bottle of Sangria that was on chill in the fridge. I found the tallest glass ever and filled it to the top. After three glasses, I started feeling the effects of it and it felt damn good. I took a quick shower and climbed into bed and tried waiting up for Remy, but he never came to the guest house. The next morning I woke up to his mother standing over me.

"You scared me, Mrs. Ramirez." I immediately sat up in the bed.

"I'm sorry for startling you. Forgive me, but I must ask you. Who are you and what do you want from my son?" I was taken aback by her bluntness.

"I don't want anything from Remy. We're just friends."

"Bullshit. I saw how you look at him. You're in love with Remy. Let me let you down easy. Remy is heir to his father's throne. The last thing he needs is a woman with a ready-made family. He needs someone pure who will give him his first born son and daughter.

As you can see he didn't come here last night. He was out with Ava, the love of his life. That is who he will marry and she will bear his children. There's a car outside waiting to take you back home. Please leave my home immediately. We're grieving. This is a time for family only."

This lady was a real live Cruella DeVille. She turned and walked out of the room. I sat there for a minute and I let what she said sink in. The tears started to fall when Magdalena came in and started removing our clothes from the dresser.

"I'll pack my own shit. I don't need you helping me." I jumped up from the bed and threw on whatever I could find then went into the room where Heaven was and I got her dressed. Once I was done packing, I dragged our bags to the door. Like she said, a driver was outside waiting for me. She was leaning against the car, drinking from a Martini glass.

"Where are we going, Mommy? Where is Remy?"

"We're going home baby. Stop asking questions. Get in the car and put on your seatbelt."

"Here is some money for your troubles." She handed me a fat envelope. I looked at it and laughed.

"I don't want your money. Keep it and buy yourself some dignity." I knocked the envelope and the glass out of her hand. I got in the car and was taken to a private air strip. I was hurt by her words and actions. Knowing that Remy was with another woman while I was there hurt my feelings. I know that I can't be mad because we're not in a relationship, but I had mixed emotions about the whole thing.

Once I made it back to Chicago, I hailed a cab and went straight to my own house. I didn't want to talk to or see anyone. I just wanted to be with my daughter. I climbed in bed and I intended on staying there for as long as I could. My mind wondered to Remy and how he would feel when he realized that I was gone. The more I thought about it, I probably should have waited until he arrived before I left. I hoped and prayed he wouldn't be mad at me.

"I miss Remy, Mommy." Heaven climbed in bed and lay on my chest.

"I miss him too, baby." I kissed her on the forehead and eventually we both drifted off to sleep with Remy on our minds.

****

The sound of someone banging on my door caused me to jump up out of my sleep. I grabbed Heaven and was ready to climb out of the window. I thought that it was Ace trying to get in. I stopped in my tracks when I heard Remy calling my name. He was telling me to open the door. I slowly made my way to the door and unlocked the many locks that I had on it. He came inside and I went and sat on the couch. We were both silent, not really knowing what to say.

"I'm sorry. My mother had no right to do what she did to you."

"Where were you all night?" All I could think about was if he had come to the guest house the night before, his mother never would have did that to me.

"I visited some old friends."

Remy couldn't even look at me, so I knew he was really with the woman his mother threw up in my face. He came and sat next to me on the couch and pulled me onto his lap. I hated that I was on the verge of tears as I thought about the way she talked to me. I made sure to never let them fall. I was over this man seeing me crying. I was so fucking tired of crying. Remy grabbed my face and kissed me. I let out a slight moan as I rubbed my fingers through his hair. He had me feeling things I've never felt before.

"I came to take you back to Mexico. I'll be there for two more weeks. I want us to spend some time together. I don't want Heaven to keep doing all this traveling so I've made arrangements for her to stay with your grandmother. She will stay at my home until we get back. I'll have security detail around the clock looking after them. Plus, your father is going to stay there as well.

"I can't go back with you. Your mother doesn't like me at all. Although we're just friends, she basically said that I wasn't good enough for you."

"First of all, you're going back with me. Second, you're going to be my future wife. Last, don't ever let anyone make you feel like you're not worthy of being in my life, mother or not. I know what's best for me and that's you and Heaven. Get your shit packed because our plane leaves in an hour."

"I'm going to go back with you but I'm telling you now, your mother better show me some respect or I'm going to forget she's your mother. You better steer clear of that bitch you were with when you left me and Heaven alone all night. I know that's who your mother wants you to be with. However, you basically just told me we're in a relationship. So I hope whatever you and her or any other female have going on, is over. I'm with you and only you and I want the same in return."

The look on Remy's face was priceless. I know that was because I'm this shy girl that never speaks up for herself, but I was dead ass serious about everything I said. The past two days I had a chance to think about things. I hardly ever spoke up for myself. I always let everybody else make decisions for me and that's how I ended up in prison. I'm not taking shit off anybody anymore. This is the beginning of a new Rose' Richards.

I'm glad to know that Remy feels that strongly about me that he would fly all the back to the Chi just to take me

Mz.Lady P

back to Mexico with him. I smiled as I packed my clothes and watched him play with Heaven. I liked how our little family was slowly but surely coming together. I feel sorry for anyone who tries to come in between us.

56

Chapter 8- Remy

Hearing Rose' stand up for herself had me harder than a motherfucker. That's the way I wanted her to be. I need a strong woman by my side to help me run my empire. Especially since I found a stipulation in my father's will. I have to be married within a year and have a son in order to inherit three hundred million dollars from my father's estate. I'm already head of his drug empire. That's more than enough money to live for the rest of my life; however, I'm entitled to my father's estate because I'm his only child.

If he wants me married within a year with a son, so be it. I would love to have me a junior running around, tearing shit up. Rose' is the only woman I want to marry and have bear my children. I have every intention on sitting her down and telling her what the deal is. I totally understand if she declines. All this shit is new to her. Plus, my mother or Ava Ortega is not making this shit easy.

Ava is the daughter of Hector Ortega who is head of the Ortega Crime Family. Over the years, him and my father were partners on several business ventures. My father and Ava's father signed contracts when we were children that we would marry each other when we became of age. Her family has been grooming her to become my wife one day. As teenagers we would have sex from time to time, but nothing more. On the other hand, our parents thought it was the beginning of something beautiful.

The night when I left Rose', I went to tell Ava and her family that there is another woman in my life that I've fallen in love with. There is no way nothing could ever happen between us. Ava was crying and all hysterical and shit, so I stayed and tried to calm her down. She tried her best to have sex with me but I knew nothing good would come of it. Her mother called my mother and that's when she went over and put Rose' out.

I was so fucked up in the head behind my mother's actions. Never in a million years did I think my mother would mistreat someone like that. All the years of being married to my father had turned her cold hearted. I put her ass in her place. I'm a grown ass man and I make all the decisions when it comes down to who I marry and who has my children. Rose' didn't deserve that shit. I fault myself because I brought her into some shit blindsided. I really felt bad knowing my mother talked to her liked she was nothing. That shit was unacceptable. That's why I hopped a flight and went right back to get my baby. I didn't realize how much she meant to me until I came back and she was gone.

*****

I watched Rose' as she walked around my villa in nothing but a tank top and boy shorts on. Her long beautiful hair was hanging in long, cascading curls. Her toes and nails were done to perfection, courtesy of the glam squad I hired to come and pamper her. I watched as different designers came in and fitted her for everything from her dress size to her panty size. She was my girl and she was used to basic shit. I'm not a basic nigga. So, I had to upgrade her to the finer things that life had to offer. When she walked in a room on my arm, she needed to make other bitches whisper, and niggas wish she was on their team. My goal was to groom her into the baddest bitch walking and to never take shit off anybody.

Later on that night, we laid in bed in complete silence. I knew that neither one of was asleep. I felt like it was the best time for me to put shit out there to her. I sat up in bed and cut the light on.

"I need to talk to you, Rose'."

"About what? Is everything okay?" She sat up and moved closer and snuggled up close to me and laid her head on her on chest.

"I'm going to keep this shit one hundred because I don't want there to be any secrets between us." At this point Rose' sat up and looked over at me with concerned eyes.

"Before I tell you what I have to say, I want you to know that whatever you choose I still want to be with you; no matter what you decide. I know that you see me as a businessman back home, but really I'm head of the Mexican Drug Cartel behind the scenes. As you know my father passed. In his will there's a stipulation. I must be married and have a son within a year of his death in order to receive my inheritance of three hundred million dollars. I want you to be my wife and give me my first born son. Please know that I'm not asking you this just to get the money. Whatever you decide I still want to build something with you." I watched as Rose' stood up and started taking off her clothes.

"Whoa! What are you doing?"

"I'm ready to give you your first born son and become the wife you need beside you." Hearing her say those words made a nigga feel good. I stopped her from taking off her clothes and pulled her back down on my lap.

"I appreciate you giving a nigga like me something so precious, but I want to make love to you *after* I give you my last name. I have nothing but the utmost respect for you, and I would be less of a man to get you pregnant without making shit official first." I could tell she was a little disappointed. As bad as I wanted to fuck the shit out of her, I knew it wasn't the right time. I was full of surprises, so we would be getting married sooner than she thought.

Chapter 9- Rose'

I keep pinching myself to see if this is a dream. Good things like this don't happen to a girl like me. I've been thinking about Remy's revelation about him being head of a cartel. A part of me knows that I shouldn't even want to deal with a man that deals drugs. The other part of me feels like Remy is the best thing for me and my daughter. I couldn't ask for a better man to be with.

As I lay in bed next to him, I know that there is no other place in the world that I would rather be. He is so damn handsome even with all the snoring he is doing. To say that I was shocked when he said he wanted to wait to have sex was an understatement. Most men would have jumped at the opportunity to have sex with me. Remy isn't like most men though. He's like Prince Charming from the hood. On one hand he has a gangster persona, and on the other hand he's sweet, gentle, and caring. Most street niggas don't possess all of those qualities.

I love that Remy knows how to separate his street life from his home life. If he would have never told me about what he really did, I would have never believed it. His honesty is another thing that has me head over hills in love with him. Remy is just too good to be true. I'm not really experienced in satisfying a man, but I want our first time to be magical. I need Neicee now more than ever. I really wish she was here. She's the only friend I have in this world. I can't wait to tell her we're getting married.

I wish I had a number on my mother. I would love to talk to her and share my good news. I want her to be proud that my life is slowly but surely getting back on the right track. I don't understand why she is so angry with me. It hurts my heart to know that she has cut me completely out of her life. Hopefully, one day soon she'll come around. I need her as my mother and Heaven needs her grandmother in her life.

*****

"Come on Remy, it's time to go." All morning he had been stalling about getting ready for his father's memorial service. The family car was outside waiting for us and Remy was not ready yet. He was sitting on the bed in nothing but a tank top and his boxers. I was fully clothed and ready to get this over with. The last person I wanted to see was his crazy ass mother. So I was ready to go support him, pay my respects and get the hell away from her.

Slowly, Remy got up from the bed and started putting on his all-black Armani suit that I had laid out for him. The stylist who came in and fitted me for my clothes schooled me about the different fashion designers. I was rocking an all-black Herve Ledger bondage dress that fit my body like a glove. A pair of all-black studded Red Bottoms graced my feet. I felt like Dorothy from the *Wizard of Oz* with these shoes on.

"You look so fucking beautiful, ma," Remy said as he wrapped his arms around my waist.

"Thank You. You look handsome as ever." I turned around and placed a kiss on his juicy lips. After kissing for a short period of time, we walked out hand in hand and got inside the family car. As we made it closer to the church, I became more nervous and couldn't sit still.

"Calm down and stop fidgeting."

Remy grabbed my hand kissed the back of it. The touch of his soft lips sent chills through my body. I swear he better stop with all this kissing before I rape his ass.

The car came to a stop and I knew we had arrived at the church. The driver opened the door for us and we stepped out. We walked hand in hand into the church. People were hugging and kissing him. They were all over him like he was a celebrity. I watched in awe at how people parted like the Red Sea as we walked down the church aisle. Once we made it to the casket, I could tell that sadness took over Remy. I watched as his tears dropped onto his father's fourteen-karat gold casket. I continued to hold to his hand and wipe his tears with the other.

"Excuse me. Can I please comfort and grieve with my son?"

His mother basically shoved me out of the way. I swear I wanted to whoop this old bitch's ass, but I couldn't let her take me out of my character. The last thing I want to do is embarrass Remy in front of his family and friends. I just stood off to the side and let them have their moment. The services were getting ready to begin and we were making our way to be seated. His mother immediately stepped in between us, blocking me from taking a seat in the front row.

"These seats are for family only. She should be seated on the other side with the guests."

"She's my family, so she will sit where ever I sit at. We had this discussion already." He pushed past his mother and I let out a sly grin at her ass. She was pissed and it showed all over her face.

We sat down and I noticed there was a beautiful, exotic looking woman sitting on the other side of him. As the Pastor spoke, I noticed that the female kept rubbing on Remy's thigh. I was getting angrier by the minute. I was glad that he kept removing her hand. This chick was the epitome of a thirsty bitch. My eyes bucked out of my head as she grabbed Remy's dick. Before I knew it I reached over Remy and grabbed her hand. I tried to break her fucking fingers. She was being messy and disrespectful and I wasn't about to let the shit fly.

"You need to keep your hands off of things that don't belong to you," I said in low tone so that I didn't cause a scene.

"Little do you know him and his dick will always belong to me. Ain't that what you promised me the other night Remy?"

"Chill the fuck out Ava!" Remy pushed her away from him hard as hell. I just turned my head and rolled my eyes. Now the shit was making sense to me now. This is the bitch that his mother wants him to marry. I have no other choice but to believe that Remy doesn't want her and he wants to be with me. However, there's something inside me that makes me think there's more to their little story than he would care to admit.

About an hour later the services were over. His father was going to be cremated so there would be no burial. I wanted to get as far away from his mother and this bitch Ava as I could. I was ready to go back to the villa we were staying in, but we went back to his mother's house for dinner.

Remy mingled with his family and friends. I sat on the couch sipping on some champagne, feeling so out of place. For some reason I started to feel like maybe I was beneath him. I stuck out like a sore thumb. If I noticed it, I was quite sure everyone else noticed.

"I need to go in my father's office and meet with some of his associates. I'll be right in the back if you need me," Remy said, as he kissed me and walked away. I wanted to object to him leaving me alone, but I knew he needed to handle his business. I sat around for about thirty minutes before I got the courage to go to the bathroom.

"Don't get too comfortable trying to live the life that was promised to me," Ava said as she stepped in front of me, blocking me from walking past.

"Please move out of my way. No one is trying to live your life. I don't even know you. Whatever went on between you and Remy is over." I tried to walk past her and she continued to block me.

"Ain't shit over until I say it's over. Remy is mine and his dick is mine. Ask him how my mouth felt the other night."

Anger came over me and before I knew it I had hit the bitch. I kept pounding her ass until I felt someone pull me off of her.

"Oh my God, she's crazy!" Ava was screaming and crying as they pulled us apart.

"What the fuck are you doing Rose'?" Remy said as he held on to me by my waist.

"She was popping off at the mouth about how she sucked your dick the other night, so I hit her ass in the mouth.

"This is why I didn't want this ghetto trash here to begin with. This is who you want to marry and give you children? No. I will not accept this. I want her out of here now. Send her ass back to Chicago with the rest of the lowlifes." His mother was consoling the bitch as blood leaked from her nose and mouth.

"All that is not necessary, ma. She hasn't done anything to you. You're only doing this to her because you want me to marry Ava. I already told you I don't love Ava and I never have. I'm a grown ass man. I choose who the fuck I marry, not you or anybody else. Rose' is going to be my wife and you will respect her and my decision."

I have never saw Remy so mad. I just wanted to get out of there. I felt so bad for letting the bitch take me there.

"I can't believe she has turned you against me. When have you ever talked to me with such disrespect?"

"You know that I love you and I would never disrespect you. How do you think I feel about the way you're behaving? I know you're grieving over Pops, but this is not the way to do it. Prior to coming home, I bragged to Rose' about how nice of a person you were. Needless to say I'm embarrassed as hell. Come on Rose', let's go." Remy grabbed my hand and we headed towards the door to leave.

"I disown you Remy. You will never see your inheritance. You're never to return to Mexico. This is no longer your home and you're no longer my son."

I couldn't believe the words his mother was saying to him and that shit made me feel even worse. Remy never even turned around to respond to the things she was saying. I squeezed his hand even tighter.

The ride back to the villa was eerily quiet. I wanted to say something but I knew he needed a moment to himself. Once we made it to the house, he went straight to the bar area and grabbed a fifth of Hennessy. Without saying a word to me, he went straight outside and slammed the patio door, causing it to shatter but not fall to the floor. I was actually scared because I've never seen him mad or angry. Not knowing what to do or say, I decided to leave him alone.

I felt so bad for him. A part of me felt like this shit was all my fault. I went upstairs to the bedroom and took a shower. Afterwards, I laid across the bed thinking of how Remy must be feeling. I really hated that I even agreed to come back. I was sitting in bed when Remy walked into the room. He was so drunk he almost fell trying to crawl in bed. I got up and started taking off his clothes. He smelled like a liquor factory. My eyes bulged out my head as I looked at his erect dick standing straight up through the slit in his boxers.

It was so damn pretty; long, thick, and black. The sight of it took my breath away. I was up close and personal with the one thing I had been craving for. My mouth salivated at the thought of pleasuring him with my mouth. All I wanted to do was make him feel better. Remy was drunk but he wasn't asleep. I decided to take a leap of faith and pray that he didn't stop me from doing what I was about to do.

I took his dick in my mouth and I slowly bobbed up and down. I was trying my best to swallow him whole. I knew that guys liked that. At first I gagged due to his length but after a minute or so, I was sucking him off like I was a pro. He was trying his best to push me off but I wouldn't stop. I just kept on sucking as if my life depended on it.

"Stop Rose'!" he yelled, as he forcefully grabbed my hair and pushed me away.

He immediately jumped up from the bed and walked out of the room, slamming the door behind him. I felt so damn stupid. I have no idea how I'm going to fix shit, and I'm the one that keeps fucking shit up.

The next morning I hid in the bedroom, afraid to come out and face him. I was so ashamed and embarrassed. I wondered if he would look at me different for what I had done. Here it is he's trying to respect me and wait until he marries me to have sex with me, and I'm acting like a common hoe. The door opened and Magdalena came in. I knew she was here to help me pack my shit.

"Mr. Ramirez wants me to assist you with packing for your departure. Your plane leaves in two hours. He wants you to be dressed and ready on time."

I didn't even say anything, I just started grabbing my suitcases and putting my clothes inside. I observed her packing all Remy's things, so I guessed that meant he was going back to Chicago as well. I couldn't wait to get home to Heaven. I missed her like crazy.

I was sad as I sat on the private plane alone. I had no idea where Remy was. The last time I had seen him was when he walked out of the room during the night. This shit was becoming too fucking stressful and being sexually frustrated wasn't helping at all. Dealing with a man like Remy was becoming more than I bargained far. I was seriously thinking of walking away from everything before I end up hurting myself behind this man. I did that shit once; I wasn't about to make the same mistake twice.

When I made it to Midway Airport, my father was already there waiting for me. I was so happy to see him. I hugged him so tight. A couple of tears fell but I hurriedly wiped them away before he saw them.

"What's good baby girl?" he said as he kissed me on the cheek.

"Nothing. I'm just happy to be back home. I missed ya'll."

"You act like you've been gone for months."

"It felt like it, Daddy."

For the rest of the drive, I stared out of the window and wondered where in the hell Remy was at.

"What are we doing at Remy's house?" I looked over at my father and he had a slick ass grin. He was up to something, I could feel it.

He never answered my question. He just parked in the driveway, got out and grabbed my luggage from the trunk. Remy had to already be here because his Range Rover was in his parking spot. We had driven it to the airport and parked it when we first went to Mexico. I'm having a hard time understanding why he left me alone and let me fly back home by myself. I walked inside and didn't speak to anyone. I know that I was rude because Remy was sitting on the couch with an Arabic Man in a business suit. I could tell that they were conducting business of some kind.

"I'll call you later when I'm on my way with Heaven." My father kissed me and left. I went upstairs and took a quicker shower. I felt so dirty after being on that damn plane all of those hours. After I was finished, I put on a pair of yoga pants and a T-shirt. At first I was going to just stay in the room, but I wasn't going to be childish about the situation. I had to stop running away from everything. I went downstairs and Remy was gone, but there was a note for me on the coffee table on top of a brief case.

I had to go to the club. I'll be back shortly. The guy that was here earlier is my jeweler, Ahmad. Look inside the briefcase. Pick whatever engagement ring you want. Money is no option. I wish we could have done this together but I know that you're in your feelings. No need to worry. Everything's cool with us. I'll see you in a little bit. Love Remy

I swear this man makes it so hard to be mad at him. I opened the case and it was filled with so many different shaped diamonds. There was one that caught my eye immediately. It was huge and iced out in pink diamonds. Placing the large ring on my finger, I instantly fell in love with it. I closed the case and put it inside Remy's office for safety purposes, laid in bed and waited for him to return home.

I stared at the ring for hours. Despite having thoughts that we were moving too fast, I knew that with Remy is where I wanted to be. Instead of being surprised by his actions, I needed to learn him and stop acting like a kid when things don't go my way. I was so anxious I needed to see Remy now and thank him properly. I threw on my Ugg boots and grabbed my car keys. I was going to the club to surprise him. I couldn't wait until he came home. I shook my head at myself.

This nigga had me way too gone and I haven't felt the 'D' yet. At least I know how it tastes.

****

"What's up Neicee boo?" I said as I walked inside the club.

"Hey bitch! Look at you over there all iced out and shit. I can't believe you're about to be Mrs. Remy Ramirez." Neicee grabbed my hand and admired my ring.

"My either girl. How are things with you and Peanut?"

"Don't even get me started on that sorry motherfucker. I swear if his dick and tongue game wasn't so good I would leave his cheating ass alone. This nigga think I don't know he still fucking that hoe, Kim. I got something for him and that bitch though, and it ain't gone be pretty. I already told Madear I'm going to hurt his ass."

"Your ass is crazy. What Madear say when you told her you was gone hurt her baby?"

"Cursed my ass out. You know how she is about Peanut and Boo."

We both laughed because Madear played no games about her boys. She raised them from birth when their mother was killed by her pimp.

"Damn baby, you wearing the shit out those pants." This dude walked past and hit me on my ass.

"Nigga, don't put you're fucking hands on me." I mushed him in the face so hard that he lost his balance and

72

fell. All the niggas he was with started laughing. He quickly jumped up in my face and tried to wrap his hand around my throat, but he didn't get a chance.

"Have you lost your motherfucking mind?" Remy said as he hit the nigga several times with his gun. Boo and Peanut jumped in and it was pandemonium. All the niggas he was with jumped in the fight. My baby was beating dude's ass until some bitch came up and swung on him.

"Oh, hell no bitch. Don't put your motherfucking hands on him." I grabbed her by her hair and we started fighting. Not long after, Neicee jumped in and we were both whooping her ass. We laid her ass clean out.

"Don't you ever put your motherfucking hands on what's mines. Now apologize to her nigga." Remy had a gun to the nigga head. Boo and Peanut had laid the other niggas out.

"I-- I-- I'm sorry," the dude managed to speak. He was bloody as hell.

"Get these bitch ass niggas out my fucking spot and I bet not ever see them up in this bitch again. I'm about to start firing motherfuckers left and right. What the fuck am I paying security for if me and my niggas got to come in here and regulate shit. Clean this motherfucker up right now."

Remy walked away and got on the elevator. I tried to follow him but Neicee stopped me.

"No, he's pissed. Let him cool down some."

"What the fuck you do to my big homie? You got that nigga going crazy," Peanut said.

"Shut the fuck up Peanut. That bitch Kim got you going crazy."

"Who the fuck you think you talking to? Don't get the shit slapped out of you, Neicee. As a matter of fact, bring your ass on. I want some pussy." He grabbed her arm and she yanked away.

"I'm not going nowhere with your cheating ass. Get the fuck out of my face nigga. Go fuck that bald headed bitch Kim!"

"Her ass is bald headed, bro?" Boo said and we all started laughing.

"Shut the fuck up nigga. Bring your ass on but leave your slick ass mouth in here. I can't get my dick sucked with all that bullshit you kicking."

"I swear if you put your dick anywhere near my mouth, I will bite the bitch off. I'm so serious Peanut."

She grabbed her coat and purse and left with him just like I knew that she would. They're about to go home and fight and fuck; that's all they do. I love them though. They're so damn comical. Boo left as well and that left me downstairs with the rest of the workers. I grabbed a broom and started cleaning up all the broken glass, wiped the bar down and cleaned off the liquor bottles.

"What the fuck are you doing, Rose'?" Remy said, as he walked towards me with his face turned up.

74

"I was just cleaning off the bar and straightening up."

"Put that fucking rag down. I can't believe you're in here cleaning up with a fifty thousand dollar ring on your fucking finger. Come on let's go home."

He walked out of the entrance and I followed behind me. He waited for me to get in my car and drive off and he did the same.

Chapter 10- Remy

Since my father's death shit has been crazy. I'm still dealing with the fact that my mother is behaving so fucking childish. Her and the bitch Ava are in cahoots together. Not to mention I now have a beef with Ava's father. Apparently my father received a nice chunk of the Ortega Family's territory in exchange for me marrying his daughter when we became of age. I'm twenty-six years old and if I haven't married the bitch Ava in all this time, that should have told them something.

Up until now, I have been running my business and my father's business without any bullshit. There's something amidst with my mother and the Ortega family, though. While I was in my father's office, I was looking at the cameras that was installed. It showed all angles of the house. I saw my mother kissing Ava's father. I was on my way out to confront her about what I had saw, but Rose' and Ava started scrapping. I'm glad Rose' can throw them hands. She better whoop her ass every time she comes with that crazy shit, and any other bitch for that matter.

I like the way Rose' is starting to come out of her shell. I'm still fucked up behind the way her mouth felt on my dick. She was sucking my shit like a porn star. I think she just puts that innocent act on. I have a funny feeling she's a fucking freak in the sheets. I hated that I had to push her away like I did, but I just want to keep my word and not have sex with her until our wedding night.

"So that's the ring you picked out, huh?"

"Yeah. I love it baby. Thank you so much for everything."

"You can have whatever you like baby." I kissed the tip of her nose as we lay in bed and cuddled.

"I'm sorry for what happened back in Mexico at your mother's house and the other thing I did. I was wrong for that."

"Let me spit some real shit to you. As long as we're together, don't ever apologize for doing what you feel. You had every right to beat Ava's ass. I'm glad you did because she was testing you. As far as that other thing, I apologize for walking away from you. I could have handled the situation better than what I did. On some real shit though, that shit was feeling good as fuck. I was about two minutes from flipping your lil ass over and giving you the dick."

"Damn! I should have held you down tighter. Can I ask you something, Remy, without you getting mad at me?"

"You can ask me anything?"

"Do you think we're moving too fast?"

"Nope. Are you having second thoughts?"

"Of course not. I would marry you right now if I could. I just feel like with everything going on with you and your mom, I don't want you to wake up one day and regret choosing me as your wife. I know that there are plenty of women out there--" Remy put his hand up and cut me off in midsentence.

"Let me stop you right there before you even let that shit slide off your tongue. I'm not interested in other women. I want you Rose'. Stop selling yourself short like you don't deserve me. I hate when you do that shit. I'm here with you and Heaven. Stop worrying about other women that are non-existent. Now let me ask you something. Are you serious about marrying me right now?" I had to sit up and look her square in her eyes, to see any hint of hesitation or doubt before she answered.

"I'm dead ass serious I want to marry you right now."

She straddled me and kissed me long and hard. I ran my fingers through her hair as I slipped my tongue in her mouth.

"It's settled then. Call your family and tell them to pack. We're going to Vegas in the morning. Everything's on me. Let me call my pilot and tell him to gas up my plane." I kissed Rose' one last time and I started making the necessary preparations.

"Oh my God! I'm getting married!"

I looked back and Rose' was jumping up and down in the bed. All I could do was smile because I loved it when I put a smile on her face.

****

"Ya'll know damn well I don't get on nobody airplanes. My blood pressure all the way up with this shit here. Peanut, let me hit that blunt baby. I need to calm my nerves."

We all laughed as Peanut handed her the blunt and she inhaled deep like the OG she was.

"I see you Madear. Take it slow though, that's some Kush," I told her.

"Nigga please. Back in my day, now that was some real weed. I don't know what this cat-piss is ya'll smoking. Wake me up when we get there. I'm headed straight to the casino."

This old lady was just too damn much for me.

Peanut and Neicee had been to the bathroom several times. We all knew what they were doing. They were officially a part of the mile high club. Boo had come with his lady friend, Honey, which was one of the strippers that worked for me. I don't know what she put on his ass but she had the little nigga's nose wide open. Dino and Heaven were knocked out. She loved her grandfather. I looked over at Rose' and she was staring out of the window in deep thought.

"Are you okay baby?"

"I'm good. I'm just ready to be your wife. I want you to make love to me all night long." She leaned over and kissed me and I needed to adjust my hard on. I was going to get blue balls fucking around with her. I couldn't get to Las Vegas fast enough. About three hours later the plane landed and we all went to our rooms to get ready and rest up for our pre-wedding dinner. We were all staying at the Bellagio.

"This room is beautiful baby. I can't wait until tomorrow night. I'll be Mrs. Remy Ramirez. That sounds so nice.

"Will I be Mrs. Remy Ramirez too?" Heaven said in her cute little voice. We both laughed.

"No baby, there will only be one Mrs. Remy Ramirez." Rose' bent down and kissed her on the cheek.

"Can Remy be my Daddy number two?"

"Of course he can," Rose' said. I wasn't sure about that number two shit. I was going to be her father and I had plans on making her legally mine. I didn't want her around the nigga Ace period. Plus, his days were numbered.

Chapter 11- Neicee

The entire time since we've been here at the hotel, Peanut has been constantly on the phone. It's really starting to irritate the shit out of me because I know it's the bitch Kim. I should have followed my first mind and got me a room by myself. I'm not beat for this shit with him.

It's sad to say that I have fallen in love with Peanut. He fucks with me hard, but I don't think the love is as strong on his end. All we do is argue and fuck. I'm so tired of that shit I don't know what to do. I knew the type of nigga I was fucking with when we first hooked up one night after the club. As much as I hate to admit it, I fucked him on the first night and that could possibly be the reason why he treats me the way that he does. As long as we're fucking we're fine. As soon as we're done, it's back to arguing and the disrespect. I watched as Peanut came out of the bathroom fully clothed.

"Where are you going?"

"I'm about to hit the casino. I'll see you at the dinner."

"Did it ever occur to you that I might want to go to casino?"

"You can go to the casino if you want to Neicee. Your ass ain't going with me though. Stop trying to make this shit out to be more than what it is."

His words hurt me to the core. Despite knowing what it is between us, his words were harsh and they hurt my feelings.

"Well damn, tell me how you really feel," I said as I got up and started putting on my clothes. I wanted to be done with his ass, but this morning I found out I was nine weeks pregnant. I wanted to tell him but after this, I'm too scared of his reaction. I went inside the bathroom and slammed the door behind me, sat on the toilet and cried for what seemed like eternity. I finally gathered myself and got ready for the dinner.

It was about two hours later when I was dressed in my all-white Akira off the shoulder mid-length dress. I decided on a pair of Michael Kors wedge heels to wear with it. As I rode the elevator down to meet up with the rest of the family, the only thing on my mind was whether or not I was keeping this baby. As soon as I stepped off of the elevator, my decision was standing in front of me. I wasn't keeping this baby.

Right there in front of everyone to see, Peanut was tonguing down the bitch Kim. I blinked the tears away. I couldn't believe he had brought this bitch to Vegas with us. That's some scandalous ass shit. I would usually go ape shit about something like this but there was no need to make myself out to be an even bigger fool than I already was. The biggest insult came when he looked me in my eyes and placed his hand on the small of her back, and they proceeded into the banquet hall of the hotel.

I felt so fucking stupid. All eyes were on me as I took my place at the table beside Rose'. I held my head down, too afraid to make eye contact with anyone. I've always been shit talking Neicee. Big bad ass Neicee. For the first time I was showing my weakness for a nigga. I hated that my broken heart was on public display for everyone to see.

"I will make that bitch leave if you want me to. Peanut is dead ass wrong. This is for family only," Rose' whispered in my ear. She grabbed my hand under the table and held it tight as she could.

"Damn nephew. I see you like your big Unc. You got both your women at the table. That's some player player shit right there. Remember how I used to be back in the day Momma?" Dino said as he bit off a piece of chicken.

"All the fuck I remember is your ass sitting up in the intensive care unit stabbed the fuck up. You played them games with Rose's mother all the time until she almost killed your stupid ass. Peanut sitting up here with Kim and Neicee at the table is not cute at all. It's actually embarrassing because I taught him better than that. As a woman, I don't see how women sit up and deal with this shit.

You ain't got to be a fool for no motherfucking body. Walk away from silly shit like this. If you ain't enough, give that nigga his walking papers. It's too much dick out here to be stuck on stupid."

I couldn't even be mad at Madear because everything she said was true. I was done with Peanut and I soon as we made it back to the Chi, I was going to the chop shop. Let Kim's baldheaded ass give him a baby.

The words that Madear had spoken gave me some confidence to hold my head high. I had to sit and think about it. Peanut was expecting me to act a donkey and when I didn't, it fucked him up in the head. Now he keeps stealing glances at me and I'm ignoring his ass.

The rest of the dinner went off without a hitch. We partied all night and celebrated Remy and Rose's new life together.   I was so happy for them. If I ever I fell in love I would want my husband to be just like Remy. He loves Rose'. He looks at her with so much love in his eyes. I'm so happy I talked both of them into taking that extra step towards being with one another.

The sound of someone knocking on my hotel room door jarred me out of my sleep. I knew it was Peanut because he walked out and left his card. I just let his ass knock all night. I hoped he knocked until his knuckles started bleeding. He can go and stay with the bitch Kim. In my heart I love that nigga, but I know he's not ready for what I'm ready for. Walking away from whatever the fuck it is we have going on is what's best for me. So if I have to go to sleep every night with tears wetting up my pillow, I will. I know my worth and I definitely deserve better.

Chapter 12- Rose'

"Come on now, Rose'. You have to stop crying while I'm doing your makeup," Honey said, as she reapplied my mascara for the third time.

"I'm sorry. My nerves are all over the place." I swear I have been crying off and on all morning. I'm scared and happy at the same time.

"Here, drink this. It will calm your nerves a little bit," Neicee said as she handed me a glass of champagne.

"Don't be over there putting all that make up on her. She don't need to be walking down the aisle looking like a two dollar hoe," Madear said as she dressed Heaven in her pretty white dress, with the tights and ruffle socks to match. My grandma has no filter. She says whatever comes to mind and has no shame once she says it.

"You look so pretty Mommy."

"Thank you, sweetie. You look pretty as well."

"Which one of ya'll is knocked up. I dreamed about fish last night."

"Not me Madear. I haven't even had sex so it's definitely not me," I said and I looked over at Honey and Neicee.

"It's not me either. Boo makes sure I take my pills faithfully."

We all looked over at Neicee at the same time. She was quiet as a church mouse, so we knew her ass was the one pregnant.

"My Peanut about to have him a little Peanut." Madear was smiling from ear to ear.

"I'm not having the baby, Madear. I can't go through all of that alone. I'm not even telling Peanut. I'm sure he wouldn't care anyway.

"I know you're upset with Peanut and you have every right to be. That baby in your stomach doesn't deserve to die because his or her parents can't get it together. Furthermore, you knew Peanut wasn't shit when you laid down with him unprotected. Might I add, it's a sin to kill a baby. On judgment day, you don't want to be standing at the pearly gates and you can't get in because you didn't follow God's plan.

A baby is a precious gift, Neicee. Just think about it before you make a decision. That's Peanut's baby too. He deserves to know."

I could tell Madear was upset. She left the bridal suite after she said her peace. She hated abortions. It was her who talked my mother and father into letting me keep Heaven.

"Why Madear always got to be right about everything?" Neicee said as she sat down and put her head in her hands.

"Don't get an abortion, Neicee. Peanut is a lot if things but he isn't a deadbeat. He'll be there for you and the baby."

"I know Rose'. That stunt he pulled last night has me all in my feelings. I'm really hurt ya'll." There was a knock at the door and Remy peeped his head in.

"No Remy, you can't see me before the wedding. It's bad luck." Honey and Neicee stood in front of me, so that he couldn't see me in my dress.

"I just wanted to tell you I love you and I can't wait to marry you."

"I love you too, and you already know what I can't wait for."

"Okay, bye Remy. That's enough before she starts crying again," Honey said as she pushed Remy out of the door. We all laughed and sipped champagne before it was time to walk down the aisle.

****

Here we are together
In a place in space
Surrounded with Love.
Here to say yes I Do
I Love You
And I want to be the only one
Cause You, You are
You are just the one
I want to spend the rest
Of my life with
You are just the one
To bring out the

Very best in ME.
You make me so happy
Happy Forever (OHHHH) we must be In Love!!!!

The sound of Pure Soul singing "We Must be in Love" echoed throughout the beautiful banquet hall as my father walked me down the aisle. Heaven looked so cute as she carried my long train. Everything was so beautiful in all white and red. There were red roses everywhere. The entire room looked as if it had been draped in diamonds.

I was surprised to see so many guests in attendance, especially since this was a last minute thing. Remy was handsome as ever in his all-white tux with just a touch of red. His dreads were freshly twisted and braided in two fishtails down his back. Boo and Peanut looked handsome as well standing next to Remy. Honey and Neicee were beautiful. They had big pretty flowers in their hair like the singer Billie Holiday. Their make-up was flawless and their long flowing dresses fit their body like a glove. I was so glad they were here to share my special day with me.

"You look beautiful baby girl. Are you ready to get married?" My dad whispered in my ear as we walked down the aisle.

"I'm ready as I'll ever be. Thanks for everything, Daddy. I love you." I kissed him on the cheek and we continued down the aisle. The closer I got to Remy the more I wanted to cry. They were happy tears though. As soon as I made it to Remy, he grabbed my face and kissed me. The whole room started clapping and whistling.

"That usually happens after you say 'I Do'," the Pastor said getting our attention. For the next ten minutes, the Pastor prayed for our union and we exchanged our vows which were off the top of both of our heads because we forgot to write them. I cried so hard when he placed a ring on Heaven's finger as well, promising to always be a good father to her. We sealed the deal with a kiss and I was officially Mrs. Remy Ramirez. Our reception was off the chain. I didn't know what to do when I saw August Alsina singing to me. Remy knows I love me some August.

Remy and his crew were getting fucked up. My Daddy was drunk as hell messing with all the young girls. Even Madear and Heaven were turning up on the dance floor. I didn't care how drunken Remy's ass got; I was getting me some dick tonight by any means necessary.

****

I stood inside the bathroom of our suite looking at myself in the mirror. I was dressed in an all-white lace La Perla thong and bra set. Remy picked it out for me to wear. I put a thin coat of M.A.C. on my lips and did a once over before I exited the bathroom. There were candles lit all over the room, as old school slow jams played on the radio. Remy was lying in bed ass hole naked, smoking on a blunt with his dick standing straight up in the air. That shit had me wet as hell. I couldn't believe this was about to happen.

91

"You look sexy as fuck Mrs. Ramirez. Now take that shit off. I want you butt ass naked." I slowly took my clothes off and seductively walked towards the bed. I crawled in between his legs and took his dick into my mouth. Slowly and methodically I made love to his dick. I was sucking as if my life depended on it.

"Ohhhh shit! Suck that dick baby, just like that."

It's crazy how I was pleasuring him and was so turned on, to the point I was moaning as well.

"Come here and sit on my face."

We were now in the sixty-nine position. The feeling of Remy's tongue darting in and out of my pussy had me going crazy. I couldn't even focus on pleasuring him because Remy was sucking the soul out of my pussy.

"Pleaaasee! Stop. I can't take it anymore." I was trying my best to get off of Remy's face.

"I thought you said you wanted me to make love to you," he managed to say with my pussy still stuffed in his mouth.

"I do," I said out breath.

"Well, ride my face right now."

He slapped me on my ass cheeks hard as hell and that made me started rocking. I felt myself exploding all over his face. Without hesitation, Remy lifted me up and laid me back on the bed. He climbed on top of me and gently parted my legs. I felt him pressing his dick into my opening and began shaking like a leaf, because I knew this shit was about to hurt.

I haven't had sex in over four years. I cringed as he slowly pushed the head in.

"Relax and let me get up in there. You want this dick right?" He was now thrusting in and out of me slowly. I nodded my head yes and without warning he pushed his entire dick inside of me. I felt like I was being ripped in two.

"Ahhhhhhhhhhh!" I screamed out in pain as he started fucking the shit out me. I was trying to grab anything that was in my reach. I had to bite his shoulders to keep from screaming out further. Eventually the pleasure sat in, and I was able to throw this pussy right back at him. We were now in the doggy style position and he was working my ass over, but I kept up with him.

"That's right; throw that ass back to daddy. That's what the fuck I'm talking about." He slapped me on both of my ass cheeks again.

"Come on and ride daddy's dick."

He laid down flat on the bed and I climbed on top of him. I slid down on him and began to rock back and forth. Not long after, I turned around and began to ride him in the reverse cowgirl position.

"Ride that shit just like that. I want you to cum all over this dick."

The way he was talking to me was driving me crazy. I sped up the pace and not long after, I came on his dick so hard it was completely covered in all my white cream. The feeling of him jerking and shaking beneath me let me know that he had cum as well. We both lay back in bed out of breath and sweating bullets.

"That was the shit. Come here, I'm ready for round two. You might as well get ready 'cause I'm about to fuck the shit out of you all night," Remy said, as he climbed on top of me and did exactly what he said he was going to do.

For the rest of the night we did just that. If I wasn't already married to this nigga I would have proposed to him, that's how good the 'D' is.

Chapter 13- Remy

It had been about a month since we tied the knot. Rose' and I were now living in our new home out in Hickory Hills, Illinois. Heaven was enrolled in a great private school, though Rose' was apprehensive about putting her in school early. I was able to persuade her to let her attend, though. Early education is important for kids Heaven's age. I wanted nothing but the best for my girls. Whatever they wanted they could have.

I hated that my businesses and my drug operation kept me away from home a lot. I could tell Rose' didn't like being away from the city and away from her family. After a while she would get used to it. I wanted my family out of the city and in a safer environment. Shit happens in the Suburbs as well, but not as much as the city. Plus, the nigga Ace was still M.I.A. Even after I had all the nigga's traps burned to the ground, he still was ghost. That nigga knows I'm at his ass for the shit he pulled with Rose'.

I have yet to hear from my mother and it's starting to get to me. We are both stubborn so I know she's back in Mexico feeling the same way. I was thinking of making an unannounced visit in the hopes that me and her could sit down and have a civilized conversation. However, I didn't want my wife to be stressed out, worried about me and what I was doing in Mexico. She had been through enough dealing with my mother and her bullshit.

I hadn't discussed it with Rose' yet, but I'm seriously thinking of handing the operation over to an associate. I'm already rich and the money is constantly pouring in. All of my businesses are doing great. I don't even want the fucking inheritance anymore. Fuck it. Once that shit left my mother's mouth, I wouldn't take that shit if she offered to me. My bank account is triple that shit anyway.

After I told Rose' about what I had to do to get the money, she was down for whatever. But I regretted that shit because she shouldn't have to be in a rush to marry or give me a son within a year. She's my wife and she has the right to choose when she gives birth. So, all I'm yelling is fuck that money. It's not worth the fucking aggravation.

Later this month there's a big meeting with my associates and I'm thinking about letting them know I'm done with the Cartel. My father would understand because he was always a family man and we came first. Now that I'm married and have a family, they come first and everything else is secondary and irrelevant.

****

"Where are you going?" I asked Rose' as she stood in her uniform from the club.

"I'm about to go in and work." She was grabbing her purse and keys like she really was going somewhere.

"Take that shit off. You no longer work there." I turned my head and focused back on the Bears vs. Packers game.

"I'm tired of just sitting in the house Remy. I miss Neicee and the other girls."

Rose' was pouting, looking good as hell at the same time. I cut the TV off so that I can have her undivided attention. I needed for her to hear me and hear me good. This would be the last time that we would have this conversation.

"You're married to me now. What the fuck I look like letting you walk around my fucking club working for me? I don't want you working. How many times do we have to have this conversation? If you want to go out, I'll take you wherever you want to go. As far as the club goes, I don't want you in there period if I'm not with you." I cut the TV back on continued watching the game.

"Just like that, huh? I have to do whatever you say. It doesn't matter what I want. I'm grown in case you forgot. If I want to go to the club without you I can." Rose' was twisting her neck and had her hands on her hips. I squeezed the bridge of my nose because I was trying my best to calm down.

"You know what, you're absolutely right. You're a grown ass woman. I'll just be glad when you start acting like one. As far as you going to the club if you want to, go ahead and try me. I'm going to come in there and drag your ass out." I got up and walked away from her ass. I went to my office so that I could calm down.

I wasn't trying to run her life. Rose' is my wife and she has to live life differently. She just doesn't understand. I hate that Rose' is kind of green to the shit that's going on in front of her. Yes, I'm a nigga that loves her and wifed her up. I'm also the same nigga that's beefing over territory and killing niggas without hesitation. That's the part of me she doesn't seem to comprehend. I have to change that because she's an easy target. Niggas will get at her because they can't get to me. I don't know what I'll do if some shit like that happens.

The sound of the security system, alerting me that the front door was open caught my attention. I jumped up and rushed to the door. All I could see was her all-black Audi driving out of the driveway. Rose' was really testing me. She was about to see a part of me she didn't know existed. I'm about to teach her ass a lesson.

Chapter 14- Rose'

I knew I was wrong for leaving like that. I regretted it once I looked in the rearview mirror and Remy was looking at me driving away. I just needed a minute to myself and out of the house. The walls were starting to close in on me. After being in jail and closed in for so long, I hate being in one space for an extended period of time.

My daily routine is getting breakfast ready for Heaven and Remy, making sure their clothes are ready for them to start the day, keeping the house clean, and making sure dinner is on the table every night when he gets home from a hard day. I'm not complaining because that's what a wife is supposed to do. I just feel like I don't have anything to do with myself.

I needed someone to talk to because Remy didn't understand. I wanted to talk to Neicee but she was at the club. I might have been mad but I wasn't stupid. I knew he would come and drag my ass out of there. I didn't want them type of problems with my husband. He's too good of a man to me for me to be blatantly disrespectful, and I love him too much for that. He gives me the world and I appreciate everything he does for me and my daughter.

I drove until I ended up at Madear's house. I hoped and prayed my father wasn't here. He had his head so far up

Remy's ass he could tell what he ate. I wasn't mad at my father though. He really loved and appreciated Remy for the things he does for all of us. My entire family loves Remy. Shit, I'm starting to think they love him more than me. Heaven loves him so much she no longer calls him Remy. That's her daddy and you can't tell her different. These days it's Ace who?

"What brings you over here on a Sunday? I got pot roast, baked macaroni, smothered cabbage, and cornbread if you're hungry." Madear was sitting on the couch watching *Law and Order: SVU*.

"I just needed to get out of the house, Madear. I'll take me a plate to go." I sat down on the couch next to her.

"Make sure you make Remy a nice plate. He works hard baby. You have to keep him fed." Once the words left her mouth I exhaled loudly in frustration.

"What happened with you and your husband?"

"Nothing."

"Don't bullshit me. He has called here several times looking for you. Why would you leave without telling him where you were going?"

"That's just it. I have to tell him everything. Everything I want to do, I can't do. The walls of my house are starting to close in on me. Day in and day out, all I do is sit in the house and take care of Remy and Heaven."

"It sounds like your wifely duties are too much on you. I'll give you a word advice. Do your job or he'll find someone to do it better. Remy needs a good strong woman by his side.

You're sitting over here complaining about nothing really. That man spoils you rotten."

"It's not nothing, Madear. Tonight I wanted to go to the club and work, but he said I couldn't. He doesn't even want me to work. He just wants me to stay home and I get tired of sitting in the house all day. I don't know anybody out there in the damn boondocks. All those uppity ass white people. I can't stand it Madear.

"Let me ask you this. Is he disrespectful to you? Does he whoop your ass for breakfast, lunch, and dinner? Is he staying out all night and coming home with the scent of another woman on him?"

"Of course not. Remy is the perfect husband."

"Exactly. You need to take your ass home and keep your husband satisfied. You know there's thots out here waiting to sink their teeth in him. As soon as you start slacking, the clean-up woman will swoop in like a thief in the night and be cooking in your kitchen. Stop running away when you have a disagreement. I know all of this is new to you, but you have to grow up.

Start handling situations like a grown woman. Learn to communicate with your husband. You have to tell Remy how you feel."

The more I sat and thought about it I knew that she was right. All of this was really unnecessary. I should have just told him how I felt instead of running away from the situation. I was dead ass wrong for my behavior. I sat and talked with Madear for a little while longer, then made us some plates and headed home.

During the drive home I couldn't help but feel bad. I was living a real life fairytale courtesy of Remy. He deserves better than me acting like a spoiled brat when I can't get my way. It's bad enough Heaven does it to him when she can't have things her way.

I sat outside of our home for a minute before I went inside. I can't believe this was our first fight. Finally, I got out of the car and went inside of the house. All the lights were out except from the light that shined from the TV. I walked into the living room and both Remy and Heaven were asleep on the couch. I picked her up and carried her to her room. I looked over my shoulder and Remy was now sitting up. I put Heaven on her pajamas and tucked her in. Once I was finished, I went back down to face the music.

"Madear sent you some food." I started unwrapping his plate and warming it up in the microwave for him. I watched from the kitchen as he got up and walked upstairs. I stopped the microwave and followed him. He was in our bedroom getting undressed and ready for bed.

"I'm sorry for leaving without telling you. It's just that I needed to get out and clear my head." I stood and watched as Remy got in bed and cut off the light, never even responding to me.

"Please say something Remy."

"There ain't shit to talk about. When I wanted to talk you didn't want to listen, so now I have no words for you. You're a grown woman. Do whatever the fuck you want to do."

Tears stung my eyes and started to fall. Remy had never raised his voice or cursed at me, so I was all in my feelings. Remy rolled over and didn't breathe another word to me. I knew he was going to be mad, but not that damn mad.

The next morning I got up to fix breakfast. To my surprise, breakfast was on the stove and Remy and Heaven were already gone. His ass could have at least said something before leaving. I ate the ham and cheese omelet he had cooked for me and sat around twiddling my thumbs until it was time to get Heaven. Once I made it to her school and picked her up, I called Remy but he didn't answer. So, I just left a voicemail and told him that I was going grocery shopping.

"How was your day, pretty girl?"

"It was okay, Mommy. I drew a picture of my family."

She handed me the picture and I felt bad for her. My poor baby was confused. In the picture it was me and her. What made me feel bad was that there was a picture of Ace and Remy holding her hands. I know it was them because she had the teacher write Daddy one and Daddy two.

"Who are these two men in this picture?"

"Those are my daddies Remy and Ace." I already knew that, I just wanted to hear her say it. I had been thinking of ways to get Ace to turn his parental rights over to Remy, so that he could legally adopt her as his own. He's done more for her in a matter of months than Ace had ever done. I'm still lost at how Ace captured her heart in a matter of days.

As we walked around the store grabbing the items we needed, I ran dead smack into a blast from my past. The bitch Diamond. At that very moment I was pissed that I had Heaven with me. I had beef with this bitch for leaving my baby all alone. She was stuck like a deer in headlights at the sight of me. I noticed that she had a small child sitting in the shopping cart. He was the splitting image of Ace. In the distance, I saw this motherfucker Ace walking down the aisle holding a little boy's hand. Once Heaven spotted him, she took off running towards him.

"Daddy! Daddy!" He picked her up and kissed her on the jaw, the whole time looking at me with those evil ass eyes of his. He made my skin crawl.

"I don't have time for this shit. Come on Jr." Diamond said as she reached out for the little boy that was walking with Ace.

"Bitch please. You had to know that one day we would cross paths. You wanted him all along with your sneaky, snakish ass. Oh yeah, don't think I forgot you left my fucking daughter on the doorstep of a strip club. Are you that jealous of her because she's his daughter?"

"Rose', get the fuck out of my face. I give less than a fuck about you or your daughter." As soon as the words left the bitch's mouth, I hit her ass in it. She was getting ready to swing back but Ace got in between us.

"This is the type of bitch you want? She mistreated Heaven and you let her. It's cool though. You might as well sign your parental rights over to Remy. He's done more for her than you ever have or will. Make sure you kiss and hug her real tight because this is the last time you will ever see her."

"Bitch, I'll kill you if you think that I'm going to let you and that nigga raise my daughter. Don't fuck with me Rose'. You know how I get down."

He had his hand wrapped around my throat and was choking the shit out of me. I managed to grab a canned good from the shelf and hit his ass in the head with it. His head started leaking instantly.

"Don't you ever put your hands on me again. Nigga, I know exactly how you get down, you woman beater, you fucking rapist, and let's not forget kidnapper. Did you know your husband raped me a couple of months ago?"

This bitch was too busy trying to apply pressure to his damn head to pay any attention to what I was saying. I grabbed my daughter's hand and got the fuck out of that store before I went to jail. On the drive home I felt kind of stupid. I had given Ace and Diamond too much of my energy. I have a new life and I can't let my past invade my future. Neither one of them are worth the headache. My husband works too hard to keep me and my daughter happy.

I was happy Remy wasn't home when I first I got there. I went straight up to my room and looked in the mirror, and Ace's handprint was on my neck. My whole neck was red. I knew Remy was going to go crazy once he saw my neck. I heard the security system alerting me that he had come inside the front door.

I heard Heaven haul ass out of her room and downstairs. Her little ass couldn't wait to tell Remy what happened. I was definitely going to telling him, I just didn't want her to tell him because that would make him madder. I sat down on the bed and waited for him to come upstairs. I could hear Heaven telling the whole story word for word. I love my baby but she's been around her Granny Madear too much. The sound of Remy coming up the stairs had me nervous as hell.

"What the fuck happened?"

Remy looked like a madman as he stormed in the bedroom. His dreads were everywhere. He was rocking an all-white thermal with a pair of Robin's on. His wheat Timbs were untied and hanging loose. He was on his thug shit today. I wanted to fuck him right there. The sound of him clearing his throat brought me back to the situation at hand.

"Nothing really. I went to the store. While I was in there I ran into Ace and Diamond with their kids. Heaven just took off towards him. Diamond said some smart shit about it, so we started arguing. Me and Diamond exchanged words and I hit her. She never got a chance to swing back because Ace stepped in between us. I told him he needed to turn over his parental rights to you. He got mad and choked me and I busted his head with a canned good. After that, I grabbed Heaven and we came straight home."

Remy was standing in the middle of our bedroom with his fists balled up, biting his lip. Yeah he was pissed.

"This is a prime motherfucking example of why I don't want you out by yourself. What if he would have kidnapped you and Heaven again? Then what?"

At this point he had walked over and turned my head from side to side, examining the bruises on my neck.

"I had to go to the store and get the items I needed for dinner. I called you but your ass is all in your feelings you sent me to voicemail as usual. I'm not about sit up here and act like I did something wrong because I went to the damn grocery store, so I could fix your fucking dinner!" I tried to walk past him, but he grabbed me and hugged me tight.

"I never said you did anything wrong. Don't you understand I would be fucked up if something happened to you and Heaven? All I'm trying to do is get you to understand that if niggas can't get to me they will get to you, including Ace's bitch ass. This is bigger than you and Heaven. Me and that nigga had beef before I even met you.

Listen to me and listen to me good Rose'. I don't want you or Heaven out alone. Going forward you will have security detail twenty-four seven. I don't want to hear no back talk or shit from you."

"Okay. I'm sorry for not listening. I love you." I kissed him and hugged him so tight.

"I love you too."

He kissed me back then he pulled away. I observed him walking into our walk-in closet and change into all black.

"Why are you changing clothes Remy?"

"I got some shit I need to handle. I'll be back later. Keep that pussy warm and wet for me until I get back."

He slapped me on my ass and left out the house. I had a really bad feeling about him changing into all black and leaving. My heart was beating so fast. I was so nervous for the rest of the night. I had to go in his weed stash and roll me a blunt, that's how scared and nervous I was.

Chapter 15- Remy

Play time was officially over for this nigga Ace. This was the last fucking time he would ever put his hands on my fucking wife. It's amazing how niggas do all this dirt close to home, never knowing when their worst nightmare will end up on their doorstep. I had my people keeping tabs on Ace since the last incident that occurred between him and Rose'. He had fucked up royally and I was about to show him I'm not to be fucked with.

I've been lying in the cut anticipating his arrival to his crib. I checked my heat to make sure the safety was off. I really had no words for his ass. My trigger finger would be doing all the talking for me. I usually let my young niggas handle shit like this, but this was personal. I had to get at this nigga myself. What type of husband or father would I be if I let another nigga murk the nigga that laid hands on my wife?

I had been sitting outside his crib for two hours when he finally pulled into his driveway. The silly ass nigga never even saw me approach his ass as he got out of his car. Without hesitation and no words spoken, I let loose on his bitch ass. I watched as his body jerked from the bullets that entered him. I didn't even stay to watch the nigga's body drop.

Before I made it to the crib, I got rid of the gun and the clothes that I had. I was glad Rose' was asleep when I made it to the crib. Had she been awake, she would have been asking question after question.

I hopped in the shower and washed away the dirt of a busy ass day. The sound of the shower door sliding open got my attention.

"Let me help you with that."

Rose' grabbed the towel from my hand and lathered it up. She started to wash my body from head to toe. The feeling of her hand along with the hot, wet towel massaging my dick had me feeling good as hell. Once she washed all the soap off of me, she dropped to her knees and took all of me into her mouth. She had adjusted the water so that it fell all over her head. The sight of her dripping wet body accompanied with the sucking and slurping sounds had me ready to explode.

"Fuckkk! Suck that dick just like that. I had to bite my bottom lip to keep from moaning out like a bitch. I grabbed the back of her head and began to fuck her mouth roughly. She was taking it all without gagging or stopping. I let loose in her mouth and she sucked until I was completely drained.

Not wanting to tap out, I had to return the favor. I kneeled down and placed her leg over my shoulder, and slowly sucked on her inner thighs until I made my way up to her pretty, pink pussy. I went straight in for the kill and began attacking her clit, sucking, licking, and biting on it. I put my entire tongue in her pussy and started to fuck her with it.

"Ohhh shit! Don't stop Remy," Rose' moaned out in pleasure, pulling me in closer.

She was grinding all on my face just like I liked. I took my fingers and inserted two of them inside of her. At the same time, I continued to suck on her clit.

"Cum for daddy right now!" I barked, but continued to make love to her pussy with my mouth.

"I'm cumming daddy!"

She was letting all her juices loose. She was squirting all over the place as I licked her clean with my tongue. Minutes later we were in bed making mad passionate love to each other. I looked up at her as she rode my dick. She was beautiful as hell. The sight of her titties bouncing up and down made me grab her and attack them. I sucked and licked on her hard nipples, flicking my tongue back and forth. She was sucking on my fingers and moaning out in pleasure. I felt my nut rising to the top and ready to explode.

"Grrrrr!" I grabbed her waist and held her in place as I let all my seeds loose inside of her. I busted a huge load. I couldn't stop shaking as I came. She didn't make it any better by bouncing up and down on my shit while I was cumming. My wife was a beast in the sheets. She had a nigga toes doing karate and throwing up gang signs.

"I should have put ring on that pussy too. That shit got a nigga sprung."

"Shut up Remy!" Rose' punched me in the chest. She was trying to act all bashful and shit. All that innocent shit is a façade. Rose' ass is a freak. I love that she's my freak and that pussy belongs to me. It's safe to say I will kill a nigga over some pussy.

Chapter 16- Rose'

It's been six months since we tied the knot and I couldn't be happier. Remy is the best thing that has ever happened to me and Heaven. I wish that we could spend more time together, but he has been extra busy opening up his new restaurant called "Reco's" in honor of his father's memory, not to mention trying to run his father's business.

I'm glad that he and his mother are back on speaking terms. Of course she still hates me and I don't give a fuck. The feelings are definitely mutual. As long as he has a relationship with her that's all that matters to me. I was surprised when I found out his mother was flying in from Mexico to attend the grand opening. I knew nothing good would come of it. One thing I did know was that she would not be disrespecting me in my home.

The grand opening of the restaurant had finally arrived. It was a casual affair, nothing fancy. Remy and I walked around and greeted our guests, making small talk and toasting to my husband's success. Peanut and Boo were in attendance. Of course they were too busy trying to get with the ladies. I was happy Neicee was due any day. I desperately needed a ladies' night with her.

"Congratulations, son; everything is so beautiful."

Cruella Deville herself was here and in the flesh. She had on the baddest Sable fur coat I had ever seen. Her diamonds shined brightly under the chandelier lights. I couldn't stand this woman but she had good ass taste. As she hugged Remy she looked at me with the most evil stare. It sent chills down my spine. There was something about this woman that didn't sit well with me. She was a snake and she didn't have Remy's best interest at hand.

"I'll be back, bae. I need to go to the bathroom." Remy looked at me and knew that I was lying. I just wanted to get away from his mother.

"Don't be gone too long," he said as he kissed the back of my hand.

I walked away and went to the bathroom, staying in there for as long as I could. Finally when I emerged, I observed a woman all over Remy. She was pulling on his dreads and whispering all in his ear. It was one thing to see her doing that, but it was another to see him smiling and acting as if he wasn't a married man.

I know that bitches flirt with him and I'm quite sure he flirts back; what nigga don't. It's disrespectful for all of this to be going on while I'm here with him. I wanted to get my coat and leave, but Madear's voice was in my head telling me to stop running from shit all the time. I quickly walked over and that's when I remembered who she was. It was the female I saw sucking his dick the day I barged in his office. I was disgusted.

"This how you doing it now? I go to the bathroom and some bitch all over you." I was so loud that all conversations around us ceased. Remy just glared at me and didn't say a word. I knew he was real mad at what I had just done. I was mad at myself when I saw his mother and Ava smirking at me. That made me even madder because I never even knew this bitch was here in Chicago.

"What the fuck are you bitches looking at?" I was on my way headed towards where they were standing, but Remy snatched me up by my arm and led me out of the restaurant.

"Either you calm down or take your ass home," Remy said through gritted teeth. I couldn't believe he was handling me like this.

"That's what you want me to do, go home so you can chill with your bitches. It's cool." I gestured for the valet to bring me my car.

"What the fuck are you talking about, Rose'? I have investors in there and I can't let anything fuck up my business ventures."

I bit my bottom lip to keep from crying. Here it was I was totally disrespected by him and all he could think about was his business ventures. He tried to hug me but I pushed his ass away from me. The valet driver handed me my keys and I got inside of my car.

The drive home was longer than usual. It was completely quiet. All I had was my thoughts and it was driving me crazy. I refused to cry. Although I wanted to, I didn't.

When I made it to the house I went straight up to my bedroom, undressed and climbed into bed. I forced myself to sleep, just wanting the night to be over. Tomorrow was a new day. It was then I remembered it was my birthday. I hadn't celebrated it in so long I actually almost let it slip past me.

The next day I woke up after twelve. I couldn't believe I had slept so long. The other side of the bed hadn't been touched. My heart started to race. I rushed around the house looking for any sign of Remy, but there was none. I went into the kitchen and there was a note telling me he had some business meetings he needed to attend. I was kind of mad he didn't even wake me up to talk about last night or to tell me Happy Birthday for that matter.

I made me a quick breakfast sandwich and went back up to bed. I was in a real funk. I just wanted to sleep the entire day away. Once I ate, I pulled the covers up over my head and attempted to go back to sleep. My cell phone was constantly going off. There were numerous messages from my family wishing me a Happy Birthday. I responded to everyone and went back to sleep. I just wanted this day to be done and over with.

Chapter 17 Remy

I had been feeling like shit ever since Rose' drove away. I never wanted her to act out like that in front of my business associates. These were rich, white men that were investors in some companies I was trying to get started. I never meant to embarrass or hurt my wife. I was dead wrong for even letting Masada get up close on me like that. I could see the hurt in her eyes and I was more embarrassed than she was.

She was ready to pop off, so I needed to remove her from the situation. I already know she'd been thinking all types of crazy shit. I came straight home and slept in the guest room. I knew she was pissed, so I wanted to give her some space to cool off.

"What's up boss man?" Boo said as he walked inside my office at the Kitty Kat.

"Shit. Finishing up this count so I can head home and make shit right with Rose'."

"I thought ya'll would be out celebrating or some shit."

"Why would be celebrating tonight?" I was completely lost to what the fuck Boo was talking about right now.

"Please tell me you didn't forget it was Rose's birthday." I laid my head back on the headrest of my chair and exhaled loudly.

"Yeah I forgot. I can't believe this. How the fuck I'm going to go home and explain to my wife I forgot her birthday.

"I don't know but you better figure out something quick. I'll finish this shit up here."

I dapped Boo up and hauled ass getting home. It was already nine at night, so everything was closed. I grabbed her some roses and some chocolates. I felt like shit giving my wife this bullshit. When I walked inside the house, Rose' and Heaven were sitting in the dining room eating cake.

"Hi Daddy. It's Mommy's birthday. We're eating her cake." I wanted to turn around and walk my ass back out the door.

"Come on Heaven. Let me clean you up. It's time for bed now," Rose' said as she got up and started cleaning off the table. She wouldn't even look at me.

"I thought we were going to watch Frozen."

"We can still watch Frozen. I just want to get all that sticky stuff off of you."

"I'll give her a bath. Go sit down and relax, it's your special day." I handed her the candy and the roses.

"It's okay, Remy, I got it. Ain't shit special about this day."

She dropped the candy and roses into the garbage can and walked away. I couldn't even be mad at her. I deserved that shit, now I just had to figure out a way to make it up to her. I followed her upstairs and took over Heaven's bath anyway. Heaven was fast asleep by the time I put her pajamas on. I went inside our bedroom and found Rose' lying in bed just staring up at the ceiling. I got undressed and climbed in bed with her.

"There is no excuse for me forgetting your birthday. I'm so sorry Rose'. I'm going to do everything in my power to make it up to you."

"Who is she Remy?"

"Who is who?

"I want to know who the bitch is you're cheating on me with. Only another bitch would be the reason you treated me so badly last night and forgot about my birthday today." Rose' was now sitting up with her back up against the headboard.

"Baby, I'm not cheating on you. I've just been overwhelmed with all my businesses and making sure shit is good in these streets. Trust and believe me there is no other bitch in my life. You and Heaven are the reason why I've been grinding so hard. I'm securing all of our futures."

"You take care of us really good and I know you're a busy man. That comes with being married to a man like you. I knew that from the beginning. I don't hold that against you and I accept what you do for a living. What I don't accept is you making me feel like I'm nothing in front of others. To everyone in that room I was nothing but another chick you fucked with, not your wife. The fact that you did it in front of your mother and two women you've dealt with before makes it worse. That chick that was all over you is the same one I saw sucking your dick.   I sat there quiet because I had forgotten all about her walking in on that shit.

"I'm sorry for making you feel like that. You know I love you more than anything in this world. Those bitches don't mean shit to me and you already know I choose you over my mother. I just didn't want you to spazz out in front of my business associates."

"You're so full of shit Remy. I couldn't spazz out in front of your business associates, but it was okay for you to openly flirt with another woman in front of them? I'm done with this conversation," Rose' said sarcastically and turned her back towards me.

"What the fuck you mean you're done with the conversation?"

"Like I said, I'm done talking Remy. This has been one of the worst days of our marriage and I just want to forget the shit."

I let her have the final say so because I was defeated at that point. There was nothing else I could say. I needed to be more cautious in regards to her feelings. I'm not cheating on her and I would never want to be blatantly disrespectful to her. Going forward I have to do a better job at protecting her heart.

The following morning I got up extra early and cooked breakfast for Rose' and Heaven. I allowed them to sleep in late so that I could go out to the mall and cop my baby something nice. She had her eyes on these Dolce and

Gabbana thigh high boots and matching bag. I had the cashier wrap them up for me. I also went to Jared's and copped her a diamond necklace with the matching tennis bracelet. When I made it back to the crib, they were still sleeping. I went inside our bedroom and placed the gifts on the side of the bed. I kissed her on the forehead and left out the room to get Heaven ready for her school day. Once she was dressed and fed, I got her off to school.

I still had another hour or two before I met with the Ortega family. A lot of shit had been brewing and I didn't want Rose' worrying about me. Rose' was fully dressed when I walked back into our home.

"Thank you for the gifts, but I need you to understand that gifts don't make me feel better. All I need is reassurance from you that everything will be okay and I'm all you need."

I was surprised when Rose' walked over and kissed me on the lips. Her lips felt good as hell. I was happy she forgave me and didn't make me suffer for forgetting her birthday.

"So, what's on your agenda today?"

"I'm about to go to the doctor with Niecee. They might be inducing her today and she didn't want to be alone."

I just shook my head because Neicee was so stubborn and refused to fuck with Peanut on any level.

"Well call me and keep me updated on things. I have a meeting and I can't be late. I'll call you when I'm out of the meeting and on my way to the club."

We kissed each other goodbye and we both headed out of the house to our car.

"Be careful, Remy. I love you."

"I love you too, Ma."

Chapter 18- Rose'

A part of me was feeling good that Remy and I weren't into it anymore. The other part of me felt like I let him off way too easy. The thought of walking around mad at him would make those bitches succeed in what they were trying to do. I lay in bed the night before, playing sleep after my conversation with Remy.

I was in deep thought and that's when shit all started to come together. Those three bitches were trying to break us up. I know that Remy's mother and Ava were working together. The other bitch whose name I still don't know, I'm not so sure of. However, the bitch has an agenda and my husband is on it. Remy belongs to me and I'll be damned if I let these hoes come in between me and him.

I know that Remy would be mad if he found out I lied to him about where I was going. Technically, I didn't lie. I am going to the doctor with Neicee, but that's later on. Right now I'm going Downtown to the Essex Inn to pay his mother a visit. It's about time we have a little sit down. I've let this old bitch get away with too much disrespect. I overheard Remy on the phone talking to her that's how I found out she was staying at the Essex Inn.

There were no parks on the street by the hotel. I drove around three times trying to find an empty space. On the fourth try is when I spotted Remy, Peanut and Boo coming out of the hotel. It looked as if they were waiting for the valet to bring their car around. The light had changed to red so I had to sit in the middle of traffic, praying Remy didn't spot my car.

The sound of gunfire caught my attention. There were all-black Lincoln Town Cars in front of my car and in the back of my car, shooting at Remy, Boo and Peanut. They were returning fire which was causing their bullets to hit my car, because I was literally caught in the middle of the crossfire. I slouched down in my seat as far as I could go. It seemed like the gunfire went on forever. I could hear the screams of the innocent people who were on the streets.

All of a sudden the bullets stopped and I heard the sound of tires screeching away. I looked towards the door of the hotel and some of the hotel employees were dead. I breathed a sigh of relief when I didn't see Remy, Boo or Peanut laid out. I would have died right there. I looked in front and in back of me and there were more dead bodies sprawled out all over the concrete.

The sound of cars honking brought me out of my trance and I immediately drove away. I was so nervous I could barely drive. I tried to call Remy numerous times without an answer. I was so scared that I was running through red lights and stop signs. It was a miracle I didn't hit anybody or get pulled over. Instead of going to Neicee's house, I went straight to my daughter's school and picked her up.

My nerves were everywhere as I pulled into my driveway. I got out and my car was riddled with bullet holes. I really didn't give a fuck. I needed to know that Remy and my cousins were okay. I sent Neicee a text letting her know something came up and I couldn't make it to her appointment. I continued to call all of their phones over and over again, and never got a response. I was trying my best not to fear the worst but that's exactly what I was doing.

Chapter 19- Remy

Shit got out of hand real quick during the meeting. Hector Ortega had the game fucked up if he thought he was going to have all of my father's territory. I went to the meeting to give him some of the territory simply because I was ready to walk away from it all. I just wanted to run my businesses and grow old with my family. This nigga Hector wanted to be greedy and take it all. The worst of it all was that my mother wanted me to turn everything over to the nigga. Her reasoning was that I was letting Rose' ruin my life and everything I had worked so hard for.

As I sat around the table in the conference room of the hotel, I thought back to the day I saw the video of him and my mother kissing. This bitch was a snake; she had turned on her own family for this man. My father worked hard to give my mother the best of everything. How could she do this to him? I flat out told the nigga hell no. He wasn't getting shit from me. Here I was giving him territory and he wanted everything. Greed is a motherfucker. I knew that there would be a war behind me going against him, but I was down for the motherfucking ride. I had no idea the war would ensue as soon as me and my niggas stepped out of the fucking hotel.

It was a miracle we made it out without a fucking graze wound. Reality set in and I knew we had to get out of the country for a minute. Not only were there prices on our heads, I was quite sure the police were looking for us. I had many associates in high places so Hector or my mother wasn't ready for the shit I had in store for them. From the moment she spoke those words of hatred to me, I knew I had to come up with a plan just in case she tried to go against me.

Peanut, Boo and I all sat on my private jet in complete silence. Reality had set in that we had to leave everything behind. It was killing me knowing that I couldn't call Rose' and let her know what was up. We couldn't even tell Dino because we knew he was weak when it came to Madear.

"I'm sorry for all this shit," I said to Boo and Peanut. The last thing I wanted to do was bring them into my Mexican Cartel bullshit.

"We good, boss. We in this shit together," Peanut said as he smoked on the blunt. I swear that's all the nigga did.

"Honey is going to kill my ass."

Boo was in love with a fucking stripper. I don't know what she did to him, but she had that little nigga eating out the palm of her hands. The thought of leaving Rose' all alone had me feeling some type of way. I had no idea how long we would be gone; I just hoped I still had a wife to go home to.

Hours later the plane landed in Rio de Janeiro. My father owned a villa there, and I had several bank accounts already set up. After some much needed rest it was back to business. The sooner we get this shit over with, the sooner we could get back home to our families. Rose' was going to rip me a new asshole for this one.

Chapter 20- Rose'

I had been nauseous and vomiting for the last week. My stomach was sore from constantly dry-heaving, and my head had been hurting non-stop. It had been two months since I'd seen or heard from Remy and I was going crazy. I was so glad my father had been around to show me how to handle all of his businesses. I hired on more staff at the club and his restaurants just to make sure everything would run smoothly.

As far as the street shit went, I had Horse handling everything. He was head of Remy's security team at the club. He also did the drops and the pickups. I was glad for all the shit I learned from Ace in regards to drugs. If I didn't, Remy wouldn't have a drug empire to come back to.

In my heart I knew they were okay. I didn't feel the need to sit around and mope. I was going to hold shit down like I'm supposed to. I was glad that I had Neicee and Honey. We had been each other's rock. We all had our fears about their safety, but we kept it to ourselves. I missed him so much and Heaven was driving me crazy asking for him. All I wanted was to hear his voice and let me know that he was okay.

Madear had worried herself sick over Boo and Peanut. The only thing that has kept her going is Lil Peanut. I was glad she had been keeping Heaven for me. That was good for me because I couldn't even sit up straight without vomiting. I hadn't been out of the bed in two days. The furthest I could make it was to the bathroom. Any bright light or sounds made my head hurt worse, so I had my room completely dark and the TV off. If I didn't get better soon I would be headed to the E.R.

*****

"Stop crying Rose'. Everything is going to be okay," Neicee said as she hugged me.

"No it won't be okay. I'm pregnant. He's supposed to be here with me." I had just found out why I was so sick. I was ten weeks pregnant. I lost all my cool and I was crying uncontrollably, knowing that Remy is nowhere to be found. I'm giving him something that he asked for and he's not here to share the good news with me.

"Man the fuck up Rose'. I have a one-month-old son that has never met his father. I'm beating myself up right now for being a bitch to him my entire pregnancy. I don't know if I'll ever see Peanut again. Please don't give up on me now, Rose'. We in this shit together. I'm here for you just like you've been here for me. Now go clean your face and I'll be outside waiting for you."

I know that Neicee is right but that doesn't make me feel any better. I could feel myself breaking down, but I knew I had to be strong; not only for Remy, but for my unborn child.

When we pulled up to the home I shared with Remy. I started to panic when I saw police cars in our driveway. I hopped out of the car before it could come to a complete stop.

"Excuse me officer. Can I help you?"

"Actually you can help by getting off my property." I looked up and Mrs. Ramirez was standing in the doorway of my home.

"This is not your home crazy bitch!" I tried charging towards her but I was stopped by the police.

"Ma'am do you have any documentation showing that you're the owner of this home."

"No I don't have any documentation in regards to the house but I do have my marriage license. This is my husband Remy Ramirez's house. I am entitled to stay here. She cannot just come here and try to put me out."

"Yes. This is my son's house but it's not in his name. It's in mine and I want you and your bastard daughter off the premises immediately. My son is nowhere to be found so there is no reason for you to be here. You have a day to remove your items from my home." She brushed pass me and got inside of a Lincoln Town car.

"Can she do this to me?"

"I'm afraid so, ma'am. I read the paperwork and her name is on the deed. Please remove your items in the allotted time. If we come back and you're still here, we will have to arrest you for trespassing." The officer tipped his hat to me and drove away in his squad car.

"I can't believe her evil ass is trying to put you out. This shit is crazy," Neicee said as we both went inside.

"Can you please help me pack some things?" I wiped the tears that were falling with the back of my hand. I walked inside our bedroom and I began packing everything of mine that I could. I made sure to get Remy's Jewelry and his safe that he kept in the room. I grabbed a pair of his boxers and a T-shirt. I needed something to remind me of him at night. I also grabbed his Givenchy cologne; I needed it. Call me crazy but I needed those things to keep me going.

I went inside his office and I found a lockbox I knew held all of his important papers. There was also another safe in there. I grabbed that as well. I was trying to find everything I knew would probably help me out. I was regretting not being more involved in Remy's personal affairs. I was his wife. There was no way in hell his mother was supposed to be able to come in and throw me out on my ass.

Once Neicee and I were finished packing up what we could, I went straight to Madear's house to put up all the safes and lockboxes. I trusted her house better than the bank. Madear would kill a bitch dead if they even thought about robbing her. I was too tired to unpack me and my daughter's things; I just wanted to lie down. The morning sickness was kicking my ass and I just knew the day's events would cause me to pass out. I didn't know how much more I could take. Little did I know shit was about to get worse for me.

Chapter 21- Ace

That nigga Remy should have made sure I was dead when he left me leaking in my driveway. I thank God every day I had on my bullet proof vest. I knew that nigga or one his flunkies was going to be coming sooner or later. Although we were having beef in the streets, I knew this nigga was doing all this over my fucking family. Rose' and Heaven are my family. What the fuck makes this nigga think he can step in and claim what the fuck belongs to me.   Hearing that she married that nigga had me ready to kill something. Now that his bitch ass has skipped town, I'm about to take his territory and his bitch. I hate that I have to hurt Rose' like this but that's the only way I can make her understand that she belongs to me.

Diamond had been walking around with her ass on her shoulders. I was sick and tired of this bitch and her smart ass mouth. I don't care how many times I go across her shit, she never shuts the fuck up. If I didn't love my sons so much, I would have been cut this bitch off. Diamond has been in her feelings ever since Rose' was released from prison. She better get with the program real fucking quick because we're about to be one big happy ass family.

******

"Hi. I'm here to pick up my daughter Heaven Black," I said to the front desk attendant at Heaven's school. For a minute she looked at me crazy. It was just my luck my baby girl came running down the hallway with her classmates when she spotted me.

"Hey Daddy! I missed you." She wrapped her arms around me and I kissed her chubby cheeks. She is the most beautiful little girl I've ever seen. I want my daughter in my life. Rose' can't keep trying to keep her from me.

"Where's Mommy?"

"She wanted me to come and pick you up."

She ran back to her classroom and got her coat and her book bag. Once I signed her out, we were on our way. I knew Rose's routine. At any moment she would be walking out of the strip club doing her daily pickups. She really was a ride or die chick. That nigga Remy was MIA and she was running his businesses for him. Word on the street was that she didn't even know where he was at.

I was glad she parked in the parking lot. I pulled in and parked right next to her. Rose' was beautiful and thick as fuck. My dick got hard just thinking of how good her pussy is. Then my jaws clenched as I remembered she had been giving it to someone else. As soon as she got by her driver's side, I hopped out of the car and stood behind her, blocking her from trying to run and put my hand over her mouth to prevent her from screaming. I turned her around so that she could see Heaven sitting in the backseat.

"Get in the car and don't try shit slick." I could feel her shaking like a leaf. I snatch her car keys and her phone from her hand and we both got inside.

"Hey Mommy. I'm so happy my number one Daddy came and got me. Now I just need to see my number two Daddy."

I couldn't believe this bitch had my daughter thinking she had two damn daddies. I wanted to knock Rose's fucking head off and she knew it. I saw that familiar fear in her eyes that I put there years ago.

"Hey Baby."

"Wipe your eyes before my daughter see you crying. I'm not about to hurt you or her. I just want to talk to you."

"Please Ace, just let us go. I won't tell nobody."

"Shut the fuck up!"

For the rest of the ride, it was silent. Heaven had fallen asleep and Rose' just stared out of the window.

"Why are you trying to keep her from me?"

Silence

"So, you don't hear me talking to you?"

"What do you want me to say Ace? Look at the crazy shit you do to me. From the moment we met you've taken everything from me. In case you forgot, I lost four years out of my life for you. How could you just leave me in jail like that? Not to mention you marry my best friend while I'm away. You kidnapped and raped me. Now here you are kidnapping me again. To answer your question, I keep her

137

away from you because you don't deserve to have her in your life. Your ass is psychotic. You don't love her. You use her to hurt me and that shit ain't right. You created her but Remy is raising her. He is Heaven's father."

"Fucking with that nigga has given you a little heart. I got just the trick for your smart mouth ass." If Rose' thought she was going to get away with telling me that nigga is Heaven's father she was in for a rude ass awakening. At first I was going to be nice but since she wants to let her mouth overload her ass, I'm about to punish her smart mouthed ass. The best part about it that nigga Remy is not around to help her.

Chapter 22- Rose'

I was so caught up in the moment of telling Ace's ass off. I didn't mean to say too much. I knew whenever he got me to wherever he was taking me, Ace was going to whoop my ass. I felt his anger radiating throughout the car. I needed to think of a way to calm him down. Before I could get my process going, we were pulling up to a beautiful home in the suburbs. I could only wonder who the fuck stayed here.

I thought that we were going to go inside of the house, but instead we went down to a door that led to the basement. All I could think of was this nigga was about to keep me and my damn daughter in a dungeon. He allowed me to enter the door first, then roughly pushed me inside and closed the door and locked it.

"Bring me my baby Ace!!" I beat and kicked on the door until I got tired. I slid down to the floor and cried. I needed Remy so bad right now. He needed to know that I was suffering without him. Why is God punishing me? I asked myself. This couldn't be life. I had been through so much in my short life. All I want is to be happy. At the rate I'm going. Happiness is something I will never get.

The sound of the door unlocking caused me to jump to my feet. Ace came in and slammed the door behind him.

"Where is Heaven?"

"She's in the house with her brothers."

"This is you and Diamond's house, Ace. Why would you bring me here?"

"This is my motherfucking house and I can bring anybody here I want. Plus, all niggas want their baby mommas under the same roof and getting along."

I already knew this fool was crazy but this shit here is just psychotic ass behavior. I became scared as his look of anger was replaced with lust. I watched as he licked his lips. I knew he was about to rape me again. The thoughts of my husband and my unborn baby flooded my mind.

"Please let me and Heaven go. I just want to go home." I started to cry and back up away from him. He quickly grabbed me by my hair and shoved me towards the bed that was in the middle of the room. I just started swinging; he was not about to rape me again without a fight.

"You want to fight back huh?" The powerful blows he was delivering to my face and head was making me woozy. After a couple of more hits all I could do was lay there.

"See what you make me do Rose'."

I could feel him pulling off my gym shoes and my leggings. I was squirming trying to get away from him. I felt him lift my arms above my head and tie them to the headboard with my leggings. Tears streamed down my face as I felt Ace's mouth on my pussy. He was taking his time eating me. He wasn't rough at all. A part of me wished he would have been rough because I knew he was trying to get me to cum.

Not long after, he climbed on top of me and began to have sex with me. He was being gentile and taking his time. I didn't understand why he was doing this to me. I closed my eyes tight and pictured it was Remy making love to me. When he came he ejaculated all over my breasts and my stomach.

"Remember how good I used to make you feel. That's all I want to do Rose'. Your pussy is still so good to me and it tastes even better." He untied me and lay next to me in the bed. I was so disgusted.

"Come on suck this dick. I want to see what that mouth do." I shook my head no.

"Please Ace don't make me do that."

He roughly grabbed my head and forced his entire dick down my throat. He began to roughly rape my mouth. It was like a scene from one of those Ebony Crime Porn movies. I was vomiting everywhere. It was like he was enjoying seeing me suffer. The roughness of it all made me feel so dirty and disgusting. When he was finished he came all over my face.

"Get the fuck up and go take a shower."

He yanked me up and pushed me into the bathroom. I cut the hot water on and let it fall over me. I couldn't help but cry. "Please Remy, I need you so bad right now." I didn't realize I said it out loud until I heard Ace speak.

"You can call that nigga all you want. Me and you both know he can't hear you. Hurry the fuck up so you can clean up all this fucking vomit. I'll bring Heaven down here in a little while. I got you and her some personal items and shit in the bags over in the closet. Don't try no slick shit Rose'. You might as well get used to this new life. I'm not letting you or my daughter go anywhere. Oh yeah, I wonder what would your husband think if he knew you were out here swallowing dicks. Smile you're on camera."

He pointed up and showed the numerous cameras that were in the room. I almost passed out. Just the thought of Remy seeing that shit made me sick to my stomach.

I cleaned up the vomit and changed the sheets on the bed. I changed into the pajama top and panties he had for me. I sat on the bed and felt hopeless. I looked around to see if there was a way to get out of the windows, but they all had bars on them. For the rest of the night I waited and waited for him to bring Heaven but that time never came. Someone was bringing me food and just sliding it in the door and leaving. I didn't know if it was Ace because the person never showed their face.

I could hear the kids above me running all around the house. I also could hear Diamond's voice. I wondered did she know I was in the basement. I watched as the nights turned to days and days turned into night. I was in prison all over again. I was losing my mind slowly but surely. My love for Remy was turning into hatred. I was blaming him for the predicament I was in. No matter what had happened, if he needed to leave me and Heaven should have been with him. He left me out here in this world all alone. Now I'm being held captive by the fucking Boogeyman himself.

Chapter 23- Remy

After being gone for three months and not hearing my wife's voice, I was on the verge of breaking down and calling her phone. I could only hope that she and Heaven were okay. The entire time we had been in Rio we had been securing our new connect and stacking our bread. Peanut and Boo were thoroughbreds and I wanted them as business partners. With them becoming my partners, that would give me more time with my family when we made it back to Chicago.

I have had nothing but time on my hands to reflect and think. My father's best friend, Dominic, was now living in Rio and he had put me up on so much shit in regards to all of my father's assets. In the amount of time I had been here, I found out that my name was on all of his policies. I was even richer than I was before I left the Chicago. I also found out that prior to my father's death, he had found out about my mother's affair with Hector Ortega. I'm still having the hardest time understanding why she would stoop so low.

Boo and Peanut were ready to head back home, but I couldn't just yet. I had unfinished business in Mexico. I was about to do some shit that I really didn't want to, but sometimes people have to become a casualty of war.

"I need to holla at ya'll for a minute," I said to Boo and Peanut, as they sat poolside chilling in the Villa that I now owned.

"What's up boss?" Boo spoke with a serious face.

"Stop it with that boss shit. We're now partners. I need ya'll to head back to the Chi. I have some unfinished business in Mexico that I must handle. Before you say anything, I have to do this shit alone." I knew they wanted to be right with me but this was my family bullshit. I had to deal with it on my own and in my own way.

"What are we supposed to tell Rose'?

"Tell her I love her and I'll be home real soon. Get packed, the jet is waiting for you. There's a duffle bag of money on board. Make sure she gets that, fam. I'll call ya'll if I have to. Other than that we won't be able to be in touch with one another. I can't have any distractions while I'm pulling off this shit. Handle shit accordingly back in the Chi." I got up and walked away before they had a chance to say anything else. I needed a clear head for what I was about to do.

Once Peanut and Boo were on the flight back to Chicago, I boarded another flight home to Mexico. I made sure to call my mother and let her know I was on my way and I had a change of heart. Rose' was no longer the woman for me.

When I made it to my mother's home, she and Ava were standing outside waiting for me. My stomach turned at the sight of both these bitches, but I had to play my part.

"I'm so glad you've come to your senses, son. I'm glad I put her and her daughter out of your home."

I almost knocked her ass out hearing her say she put them out. Yes her name was on the deed, but I paid for the fucking house in cash and furnished it. She had no right to put my wife out of the home I had given her. I had to call Peanut and Boo. It had been months since we left. Where the fuck was she staying at? I received my mother's hug and hugged her back."

"I was so worried about you. I'm so happy you're here. Is it true Remy? Are we going to be together now?" I hated to toy with Ava's feelings but she was weak for a nigga. What she didn't know was that she would play the biggest part in bringing her father down. From the twinkle in her eyes, I knew this shit was going to be like taking candy from a baby.

"Yeah Ava, we're going to be together. I'm sorry for everything." I pulled her into my embrace and kissed her passionately. Ava was a bad bitch. She had a banging ass body so it was easy for me to play my role. I hated that eventually I would have to have sex with her. That meant that I would have to cheat on Rose'. That's the last thing I want to do in this world. This shit is business nothing personal.

Chapter 24- Neicee

"Please stop crying Lil Peanut." Madear had spoiled my baby rotten. Now all he wanted me to do was sit up and hold his ass all day long. He was driving me crazy with all this crying. I knew that he was also missing his Madear. With Rose, Peanut and Boo missing she just couldn't take it. All the worrying had caused her blood pressure to skyrocket which caused her to have a stroke. She's going to be okay. She just needs to go to a rehabilitation center.

I'm so stressed out worried about Rose' and Heaven. I don't know if she just up and skipped town or if that crazy ass Ace has kidnapped her again. Dino has turned into a real alchy these days. I don't know what would happen if me and Honey hadn't been holding shit together. Remy's blocks had been completely taken over by Ace's crew. That nigga had been MIA.

Shit was going smooth until all of our muscle had been killed. Basically with Remy, Peanut, and Boo being MIA, there was a hostile takeover and Ace was now that nigga, with his coward ass.

Everyday I've hoped that they're okay. My son is now five months old and is the splitting image of Peanut. I get teary eyed sometimes looking at him. In my heart I know that I love that man. I regret being mad at Peanut for my entire pregnancy. I was just so mad at him for treating me like he was for that bitch Kim. Life is too short to walk around holding grudges.

If I could just hear his voice or kiss his big ass lips one more time. I laugh to myself as I think about our arguments and fights. Tears were about to fall from my eyes when I heard my front door open and close. I grabbed my gun from my dresser and was ready to blow a motherfucker's head off. All the bullshit that was going on had me paranoid as hell. I was shooting first and getting the fuck out of dodge.

"Yo! Neicee are you in here."

"Give me one good reason why I shouldn't shoot your black ass right now." I had my gun aimed at Peanut's stupid ass.

"Because I'm your baby daddy and you wouldn't be able to get no more of this dick." Peanut walked towards me and took the gun out of my hand. I cried so hard as we hugged in silence for what seemed like eternity. Reality set in and that's when I went from 0 to 100 real quick on his dumb ass.

"You motherfucker! Do you have any idea what we've been going through here? How could you just up and leave us like that. Where the fuck have you been?"

Peanut was trying his best to block the blows but I wasn't letting up. I wanted to kill his ass. The only thing that stopped me from hitting was my son crying. He brushed past me and walked to my bedroom. I went and sat on the couch.

He needed time to bond with his son. I still can't believe he missed out on the first five months of his life.

"What the hell have you been feeding my son?"

My coochie got wet instantly looking at my baby daddy. I hadn't had any since the wedding dinner in Vegas. Wherever the fuck he was I could tell he had been getting money. This nigga was iced the fuck out wearing a Robin outfit. He even had the matching hat on.

"I haven't been feeding him anything. Madear has been giving him greens and cornbread." The mention of her name brought our realities back to the present. I didn't know how I was going to tell him Rose' was missing and Madear was sick.

"What did you name him?"

"Parrish Demond Richards, Jr."

"Thanks for giving me my junior. I know I fucked up but I'm here now and I want us to be together. Pack ya'll some clothes. Let's go see Madear. I know she been going crazy. First we need to go and see Rose' and Heaven.

"Peanut, a lot of shit had went down since ya'll been gone. Rose' and Heaven are missing. They've been gone for almost three months. Madear was so worried about her grandkids being missing that she had a stroke. She's in the rehabilitation center. Dino, Honey and I have been running all the businesses. We tried to keep the blocks running but Ace and his crew took them all. They killed all the muscle we had including Horse. We need to find Rose' she's pregnant"

"That nigga has her and Heaven. We need to get her back home before Remy finds out." Peanut was pacing back and forth in deep thought.

"Where is Remy? We have to tell him."

"Don't worry about all that and don't start asking questions, Neicee. Pack ya'll shit and let's go. I got things to do and niggas to murk."

"What the fuck you mean don't worry about it? While you niggas been gone we been out here going through it. I got mad respect for Remy but he needs to bring his ass home and find my friend. Peanut he has her. I know he does." I was now crying hysterically because I wanted my friend and my niece. I didn't have a friend before meeting Rose'. She has been through so much. She doesn't deserve this shit.

"Stop crying, bae. Just pack and let's get out of here. When we get to our new crib and get settled in, I'll explain everything. I just need to go check on my Granny right now. You've been holding a nigga down for this long, I just need you ride for me just a little while longer. I promise you we're going to get Rose' and Heaven back." Peanut kissed my forehead and gestured for me to get our things together. I didn't know where we were going. The only thing I knew was that I never wanted me or my son to be away from him again.

*****

The next day I just rode around trying to clear my head. Peanut was making me mad because I knew he was hiding some shit from me. All this time he's been gone. I think I deserve more than all these short ass answers he's giving me. He pissed me off so bad, whispering all in the phone and shit. I grabbed my keys and left. He needed to spend time with his son anyway. I received a call from Honey so I went to pick her up. From the sound of her voice she was pissed at Boo as well.

"What's up bitch?" I said as Honey got inside of my car.

"I'm so happy you came and got me. If I would have stayed in that house one more minute with Boo I was going to kill his ass," she said as she flamed up a Kush blunt.

"Tell me about it. Peanut acting all secretive and shit. I'm constantly asking where the fuck is Remy. All he does is change the conversation on my ass. Those niggas hiding some shit, I can feel it."

"That nigga Boo made me so mad last night I pissed in his bath water."

"You did what?" I was laughing so fucking hard at Honey's ass. The look on her face let me know that she was dead ass serious.

"He told me to run him a hot bath because he was exhausted. So, I pissed in his bath water because he pissed me off. My friend missing and these niggas playing in their motherfucking ass."

"Your ass better hope Boo don't find out you did that nasty shit. He gone whoop your ass Honey."

"That nigga ain't crazy. The last time he called himself putting his hands on me, I put matches in between his toes while he was asleep and lit those bitches. That nigga had blisters for days. I fights real dirty." Honey sat back and puffed on the blunt like it was nothing.

"Pass me the blunt, bitch. Your ass is crazy."

We continued to drive and ended up on Pulaski and Keeler at the light. We were both quiet because we were high as a kite. I looked to my right and I almost lost it. It was Ace and he was walking with some female I assumed to be his wife. She had some kids with her. I couldn't get a good look because a car was blocking the kids. I pulled over into a parking lot where a laundromat was at. They all had went into the barbershop across the street.

"Did you see that nigga Ace?" I elbowed Honey trying to get her attention. Her ass was on Jupiter somewhere.

"Hell naw. I'm over here in my zone. I wonder where Boo get that shit from…got me higher than giraffe's pussy over here."

"I need you to focus right now. I just saw Ace and a bitch with some kids go inside the barbershop. We're going to wait right here until they come out. I want to follow their ass. Hopefully they lead us to their home. In my heart I know that nigga has my friend somewhere."

"Let's call Boo and Peanut and let them know what's up."

"No, we can't do that. They will kill Ace as without a doubt. I need him alive for the time being. Plus, I'm not thinking about their asses. It's our turn to keep some shit from them. Now shake that high off bitch. I have a gut wrenching feeling shit is about to get real. I got my gun under my seat. Did you bring your heat with you?"

"Don't insult me, Neicee. I never leave home without Clyde."

Honey pulled her pearl handled Ruger from her purse and kissed it. When I first met Honey, I thought she was nothing but a basic stripper bitch. Lord was I wrong. This bitch is psycho, but I love it.

About an hour later they all emerged from the Barbershop. Tears welled up in my eyes as I saw Heaven holding Ace's hand.

"Oh my God! Heaven is with them." Tears were streaming down my face because if he had Heaven with him and his wife, where the fuck could Rose' be?"

"Calm down Neicee. We're about to follow their asses. One thing for sure and two for certain, we're not going home without Heaven."

We followed them all the way out to the fucking suburbs and parked up the street from the house they went in. We could see everything going on from where we were parked. Twenty minutes after parking, Ace came out and went down some stairs, staying in there for about an hour. Finally he emerged, hopped in his Range and left.

"Let's go knock on the door, whoop that bitch and get Heaven out of there," Honey said zipping up her coat and putting her gun in the small of her back

"Let's do this shit." We both were getting ready to emerge when Diamond bursts out of the front door and went down the same stairs Ace had went down. Something had to be down those stairs and we were about to find out what the fuck it was.

Chapter 25- Diamond

I guess the saying you get what you ask for is so true. The minute I found out Rose' was fucking Ace, I just had to have him. I always had a crush on him. To know that he was showing Rose' all the attention I wanted him to show me, had a bitch jealous. So, I vowed to take that nigga from her. Had I known what came with fucking this nigga, I would have let him and her ass ride off into the fucking sunset.

Now I'm married with two kids by a nigga that don't give a fuck about me or my kids. The only thing he's worried about is the little bitch Heaven with her spoiled ass. I will be so glad when her momma comes and get her ass. What type of mother leaves her child for months and doesn't call or check on her? It's time for her ass to go. She's causing a problem for me in my household.

Ace has been acting so ugly towards me since the bitch Rose' got out of jail. If I find out this nigga been cheating on me with that bitch, I'm killing him and her ass. I hate that bitch so much. It's sad because Rose' has never did anything to me. I hate her because he will never love me the way he loves her. You would think after being shot by her husband he would go sit his stupid ass down somewhere. I'm at my wits fucking end. I don't know how much more I can take being married to this nigga.

****

"How much longer is she going to be here Ace?" We had just come back from the barbershop and he was getting ready to leave again. He's always gone. I was tired of him leaving his fucking daughter on me.

"As long as I want her to be. Why do you keep asking me that?"

"Because I want to know. Let me find out!"

"Let you out find out what? Don't get fucked up."

"You know what, I'm tired of this shit. I'm done. When you leave out that door, take your daughter with you. When you bring your black ass back don't expect for me to be here. Me and my sons will be gone. It's not like you give a fuck about us anyway." I ran upstairs and went straight to my bedroom and slammed the door. I sat on the bed and cried. I hated that I loved his ass but I knew I needed to leave him. As soon as I got up to grab my luggage, the bedroom door swung open and Ace was standing there with his thick ass belt in his hand.

"I've been sparing your smart mouthed ass for a minute. You forgot who the fuck I am but let me remind you bitch."

As soon as the words left his mouth, the first hit from the belt slapped me across the face. I was trying my best to stop the belt but nothing helped.

"Ahhhhhhh!" I screamed as he ripped my dress off of me. At the same time he continued to whoop me with the belt. I could feel the welts all over my body. He dropped the belt and started punching me in face.

"Please stop Ace. I'm sorry baby. I won't talk smart anymore." I was begging and pleading as I balled up in a tight ball.

"Your mouth should only be made for one thing and that's sucking my dick. Now open your mouth so I can really shut you the fuck up. You bet not bite my shit."

My nose and mouth was bleeding. He yanked me up by my hair and started slapping me all in my face with his dick. He basically pried my mouth open. I didn't want him to hit me anymore, so I sucked his dick like it was going out of style. As soon as he finished, he let loose all over my face. I cried as he zipped his pants up and walked out of the room.

I ran in the bathroom and jumped in the shower, letting all the hot water run all over me. The pain from the welts was nothing compared to the pain in my heart. Everything I ever felt for Ace was gone in an instant. He doesn't love me anymore and that shit hurts.

I'm cool with that because love doesn't hurt and that nigga has hurt me for the last time. As I sat on the side of my bed trying to figure out my next move, the bedroom door opened and it was Heaven. She was crying so bad I felt sorry for her. My sons were probably locked in their room. They're used to these episodes between me and their father.

"I want my Mommy. Can you please take me downstairs to her?" She wiped snot from her nose with her shirt.

"I'm sorry Heaven. Your mommy isn't downstairs. When your Daddy comes back, he'll let you call her okay."

"She's in the basement. That's where Daddy makes her stay." I was in utter disbelief at what this baby was telling me.

"Stay here Heaven. I'm going to see if your mommy is downstairs."

"Don't tell Daddy I told you. He said he would kill my mommy if I told."

I pulled her in and hugged her tight. I couldn't believe this shit. No wonder Ace had been spending so much time down there. I had to see the shit with my own eyes. I didn't want to believe he had been holding this girl in our home where our children sleep.

I sprinted down the stairs and made my out of the door. I made sure to grab Ace's keys off the hook. He slipped and left the key to the basement. He never left that key and I was about to find out why. He forbade me from ever going inside the basement because it was his man cave. There was no entry on the inside of the house. I had to go outside to get in, that was the only way we could get inside the basement.

I let out a deep breath before sticking the key in the lock. I went inside and I almost fainted. Rose' was tied to the bed. She looked so exhausted. My eyes bulged as I looked at her stomach; it was huge. I covered my mouth to stifle the scream that threatened to escape my mouth. Rose' was just staring at me with tears streaming down her face.

"I'm so sorry. I didn't know. I didn't know you were down here." I was trying my best to untie her. I had to get her out of here before Ace came back.

"It's okay Diamond. I know you didn't know. Are you okay?" I never even got a chance to respond because the door was being kicked in. I almost shitted in the floor thinking that it was Ace.

"Back the fuck up Boo Boo Kitty before I put hole in your fucking head," a woman with long Honey Blonde hair said as she pointed her gun at me.

"What the fuck have y'all been doing to her?" another woman said with her gun pointed at me as well. She rushed towards me and tackled me to the floor and we began to fight.

"No! Neicee. Let her go. She didn't know he had me down here. Untie me right now. Honey go get my baby from upstairs!" Rose' said and her friend stopped whooping my ass. I jumped up off of the floor and we both started untying her.

"Fuck her stupid ass. I know damn well she didn't believe you would just drop your daughter off to her and her psycho ass husband."

I didn't even respond because my real stupid ass did think that.

"Please get me and my daughter out of here before he comes back. Diamond, we have our differences but you need to pack your shit and get away from him. Ace is a monster. He should not be around children period."

"I'm leaving but not before I fuck his life up."

"Come on, let's get the fuck out of here," the chick with the blonde hair said, holding Heaven.

Rose' got up and rushed towards her daughter. They all left without a word. I remembered Ace kept kilos upstairs in the safe. I sprang into action. I went back upstairs to the house and started filling a duffle bag up with as much cash as I could. I didn't bother to grab any clothes. I could always get me and the boys' new clothes when we made it to Dallas, Texas where my mother now lived. I hopped in my car, called the police and told them Ace's name and everything else I knew about his ass. I made sure to strategically place kilos throughout the house. He didn't deserve his freedom. He was about to go away for a long time.

Chapter 26- Rose'

The feeling of my baby moving around in my stomach was the only thing that was keeping me going. I was unsure of how long I had been down in the basement. From the looks of my stomach, it had to have been quite some time. I was so scared when Ace realized I was pregnant. I just knew he was going to beat the baby out of me, but he didn't; that only made him want to have sex with me more. He said that pregnant pussy was the best.

I hated having sex with him. On the other hand I was glad he was gentle and not raping me. Over the course of the time I had been locked up in the basement, Ace had softened up. He still kept me tied up when he left. He spent more time with me than he did upstairs with his family. It was still so hard for me to believe Diamond didn't know that I was in her fucking basement.

Every day I tried to figure out how the fuck I was going to get out of there. Every so often, Ace would bring Heaven downstairs to spend time with me and I was happy for that. In reality, it didn't matter that Ace was being nice to me. The fact remained the same: he was holding me against my will and using our daughter as leverage against me. All I wanted was for Remy to come rescue me, like he had done so many times before.

I used to cry every day for him. Now I can't bring myself to cry because I was all cried out. Ace was trying to break me but I wasn't broken. Remy came in like a thief in the night and stole my heart only to disappear and leave me behind. Every day I wondered did Remy come back home and if he was out looking for me. That shit was just wishful thinking. If he was out looking for me, there is no way I would have still been in that basement all that time.

Everything happened so fast. One minute I was tied up, the next minute I was in the hospital being looked at. Due to the excessive rough sex I had endured on a daily basis, I set up a really bad bacterial infection in my womb. If there was any chance to save the baby I would have to have a caesarean section immediately.

I was so grateful to Honey and Neicee, but it was something they weren't telling me. I could see it in their eyes. I was glad my father had made it to the hospital to hold my hand during the procedure. That night I gave birth to Remy Ramirez Jr. I didn't get a chance to see him because he was rushed to the Neonatal Intensive Care Unit because he wasn't breathing. I was so sad but glad I had my father there with me. He always knows just what to say to make me feel better.

*****

I was in the hospital for about a week before it was time to be released. The last thing I wanted to do was leave my son in the hospital, but I had no other choice. He was only one pound when he was born. He was so tiny he could fit in the palm of my hand. His lungs weren't developing like they wanted them to. The doctor had told me to prepare myself in the event he didn't make it, but I wasn't claiming that.

My son was a fighter just like his momma. He was the splitting image of Remy. He was going to be a heartbreaker just like his half-breed ass Daddy. Just looking at him makes me sad. I was starting to lose faith that he was still alive. Remy loves me and Heaven too much to stay away this long. Plus, he would never miss the birth of his born son.

******

"I'm so happy you're home. I missed you and my grandbaby so much," my Daddy said to me as he drove me home from the hospital.

"I'm glad to be home as well. I just wished the baby could have come home with me."

"It's okay. He'll be home as soon as he gets strong enough."

When we made it to Madear's house, there were a lot of cars parked outside. Our whole family was there since Madear had finally been released from the rehabilitation hospital. I hated that she worried herself sick over her grandchildren. I walked inside the house and I was in shock, seeing Peanut and Boo sitting at the dining room table eating. Honey and Neicee were also sitting at the table. I found it funny that they wouldn't make eye contact with me.

Peanut and Boo got up and hugged me.

"Where is Remy?" I looked around the room and everybody was quiet.

"I know you motherfuckers hear me! Where the fuck is Remy at?"

"We don't know, cuz," Peanut and Boo said in unison.

"I don't believe you motherfuckers. Ya'll are lying to me. Do you have any idea what I've been through? Ace had me and our daughter in a fucking basement for months. He made me do all types of disgusting shit to him every day. I just gave birth to his son who might not make it. I thought ya'll was my family. I'm so over this shit. Come on Heaven."

"Don't you leave out of this house Rose'. I know you're mad but that is not the way to do it. Go lie down in my bed and cool off. You just had a baby. Calm down before you have a setback," Madear said as she took Heaven's hand and led her to the table.

I went to the back and slammed the door as hard as I could. I never wanted this life. A part of me wishes I would have done that last year in jail. Anything is better than getting raped, kidnapped, and abandoned by your fucking husband.

"Can we please talk Rose'?" Peanut asked as he peeked his head in the door.

"If you're not coming in here to tell me where Remy is, don't come in here at all." He came in and Boo followed him.

"He's in Mexico."

"Is that where ya'll have been all this time? Wait a minute. What the fuck is he doing in Mexico?"

"Hell naw. We were in Rio. Some shit went down at the meeting we went to with the Ortega family. We had to take flight. I'm sorry we didn't reach out to you but it was for the best."

"Who was it best for, huh? What ya'll did was selfish as hell to me, Honey, Neicee, Madear, Heaven and Lil Peanut. Shit has been all fucked up here. I'm glad ya'll are okay but I'm having a big problem with Remy being in Mexico and not here with his family. I advise ya'll to call that motherfucker and tell him to bring his ass home to his family or when he does decide to grace us with his presence, he won't have a family to come home to."

I left both of their asses standing there looking stupid. I meant every fucking word I said. Remy got me all the way fucked up. As the night went on, Peanut and Boo gave me a duffle bag with a million dollars in it. I just shook my head because Remy thought that money made every fucking thing okay. I took it though. I'm mad at his ass, but not mad enough not to spend his fucking money.

Later that night I tossed and I turned. I couldn't sleep for shit in the world. I just kept thinking what was so important for Remy to go to Mexico. I wasn't insecure or anything, but the fact that Ava and his snake ass mother was in Mexico had me wondering what was going on out there. Right then and there I made the decision to go and get my fucking husband from Mexico. He was coming home if I had to drag his ass back by his dreads. I had this gut feeling something wasn't right.

I didn't trust that bitch Ava or his mother. Her house was going to be the first stop I made. I never got a chance to put the old bitch in her place. Better let then never. The bitch didn't have to like me but she was going to respect me. I got up and started making arrangements to fly out there in the next two days. I needed to make sure my son had around the clock care and Heaven was well protected. Ace was in jail but I was taking all precautions to make sure she was safe.

I called Honey and Neicee and told them what my plan was. I made them bitches promise not to tell Boo and Peanut. If they knew what I was about to do, they would snap the fuck out. I can't keep sitting around crying and feeling sorry for myself. It's time to boss the fuck up and take action.

The entire plane ride to Mexico had me nervous hell. I kept thinking what I would say or do once I saw Remy. I just really wanted to feel his strong arms wrapped around my body. I needed for him to tell me that everything was going to be okay. Since the day I met him, I always felt so secure. As long as I had Remy in my life I could conquer anything.

It was amazing how we met and fell in love so fast. Even after I found out what he really did, I still wanted to be in his world. It didn't matter to me. I had my reservations about moving too fast but he assured me that everything would be okay. Everything was okay, until he skipped town without as much as a phone call. I can't believe I just hopped on a plane and left my babies, to find their father. Like I said before, love has a way of making you do some crazy shit.

When the plane finally landed, I checked into a nearby hotel before taking the boat ride to his mother's estate. I needed to look my best when I saw my husband. The baby had put some pounds on me in all of the right places. I decided to wear an all-black Christian Dior jumpsuit with a pair of peep-toe Red Bottoms. I flat ironed my hair bone straight. I love that I had length and I could rock my own hair.

My eyelashes and eyebrows were on fleek. My hands and feet were done to perfection. I must say I was a bad bitch walking. Remy was definitely about to see what he was missing.

I paid the owner of the boat to wait at the dock for me just in case I couldn't find Remy and I had to go back to the hotel. There was no way in hell I could stay at his mother's home. Once the boat docked, I couldn't help but to notice the other boats that were docked. I observed numerous people in black tie attire. They were all so beautiful. I was glad I was dressed for the occasion so I blended right in.

After walking a short distance, I realized all of the people were going to the Ramirez estate. The entire house was lit up with special lighting. There were balloons and banners that read "Congratulations" everywhere. I wondered what in the hell they were celebrating. There was security all around. As I made my way to the front of the house, there

169

were several people walking inside. I walked in with them so that I wouldn't be stopped and asked any questions. The sight of Remy standing next to Ava with his hands around her waist made me sick to my stomach.

"I would like to propose a toast to my son and future daughter-in-law. Congratulations on your engagement," his mother said as she held her champagne glass up high. The entire room held their glasses in the air and saluted them as well. I know damn well I must be deaf because I know I didn't hear what the fuck I thought I did.

As a waiter walked past, I grabbed two flutes of champagne and drank them straight down. I stayed back in the cut and watched as her and Remy exchanged kisses and smiley faces with one another. I chilled in the cut taking in everything. I was definitely about to crash this motherfucking celebration. Remy was dressed in a nice tux, and the bitch Ava had on some shit that looked like that robe Kim Kardashian wore to the Grammys. They looked like the happy fucking couple; too bad that shit wasn't going to last long.

"I would like to thank everybody for coming to celebrate my engagement to the love of my life. I've loved this man since we were kids and now we're about to be one. I couldn't ask for a better man to be my husband and the father of my children," Ava said and she reached over and kissed Remy on the lips. When he kissed the bitch back, I knew that was my cue to turn the fuck up.

I clapped as I walked through the crowd and stepped in front of them. To say Remy looked like a deer in headlights would be an understatement. The whole room was quiet wondering who in the hell was this bitch.

"If had known this was an engagement party, I would have a brought a gift. Then again, I'm the gift that keeps on giving, ain't that right Mr. Ramirez? Forgive me everybody. Allow me to introduce myself. I'm Rose' Ramirez, Remy's wife and mother to his three-week-old son, Remy Ramirez, Jr.

In case you don't understand what I'm saying, he's already married so there is no way these two are getting married. Last time I checked, I hadn't received my divorce papers, so all this shit is a waste of time. "

"Rose' baby, it's not what it looks like." He walked towards me and I took a couple of steps backwards. He was just all over that bitch. I didn't want his slimy ass hands on me.

"It's exactly what it looks like, Remy. How could you do this to me? While you're here living a double life, our son is back home fighting for his life." I could tell the mention of us having a son shocked him.

"Who the fuck let this bitch in here? She's trespassing. I want her removed immediately," his mother said and all the security walked towards me and started grabbing me.

"Get your fucking hands off of my wife!" Remy said as he started pushing all of the security off of me and grabbing me at the same time.

"What is going on Remy? You said things were over between you and her. All this time you've been here with me, I thought you loved me." Ava was crying looking ugly as hell. I wanted to cry as well, but her or his mother wouldn't get to see me hurt.

"I knew you were up to no fucking good. I'm going to kill you for fucking over my daughter and my money."

I turned around and it was Hector Ortega with some of his men standing behind me. The sound of gunfire erupted and I saw a bullet hit Hector in the forehead.

"Bitch ass nigga!" I heard Remy say. That let me know he was the one who shot Hector. The guests were running and screaming like crazy.

"Ahhhh!" I screamed as I was pushed on the floor from behind. I was trying to get up but I couldn't.

"When I rise up, I want you to run out of here. I'll cover you. Mr. Ramirez will get in contact with you as soon as he can. You're even more beautiful than he said you were, Mrs. Ramirez. Now get out of here!" the unknown husky voice of a man whispered in my ear.

Gunfire was still erupting all around me. I managed to look behind me and saw Remy and his men shooting at Hector's men. I looked to my left and his mother was laid out on the floor with a gunshot wound to the head. I hurried up and ran out of the door, only to be snatched inside of a damn black Expedition. I fought and screamed trying to get away from whoever was holding me. I have the worst fucking luck ever. Who in the fuck gets kidnapped three times in a year? Me, that's who.

"Calm down, Mrs. Ramirez. We are under strict orders from your husband and our boss to take you somewhere safe."

"I don't give a fuck what he told you to do. Let me out of here so I can go home. Fuck Remy!"

"You're far too beautiful to have such a potty mouth."

"Don't fucking play with me right now. I'm not in the mood to be patronized. Let me the fuck out of this truck." No matter how much I acted a fool, they ignored my ass. Shortly after, I was being led into a damn house and then locked inside of a room. I can't believe Remy was holding me hostage now. I really need to reevaluate the men I fall in love with and have kids with.

Chapter 27- Remy

"Fuck! Can somebody please help me to understand how my fucking wife got pass security?

"Sorry boss, I fucked up," my head of security said.

"You damn right you fucked up. Lucky for you my wife wasn't harmed or you would be laid out with the rest of these motherfuckers. I want this bitch burned to the ground." I looked around at the numerous bodies that were sprawled out all over the floor. The majority of the men were Hector's men. I looked over at my mother's body and asked the Lord for forgiveness.

My mother had been against me and my father from the jump. She had been having an affair with Hector for many years. It was her who was always in my father's ear about giving some of his territory to Hector. My father thought it was because she wanted him to be at home with us more, but in reality she was slowly and methodically helping the nigga take everything my father had worked for.

The worst of it all was Magdalena telling me that my mother had purposely gave my father excessive amounts of Morphine which killed him. That hurt my heart so bad. My father was a great husband to her selfish ass. In return she slept with the enemy and killed the best father in the world.

So, it's fuck her evil ass. I hope and pray she rots in hell because that's exactly where she's going.

The entire time that I had been in Mexico, I managed to get back in my mother's good graces. I was able to get codes to some safes that were located in his office. I ran across numerous deeds to homes we had all over the world, not to mention a shitload of bank statements linked to offshore accounts. Looking over my father's will, I found that he had left everything to me. My mother wasn't getting shit. That's why she was against me from the jump. In the event of my untimely death, she would inherit everything. The bitch Ava was in on it too. She managed to get away in the midst of all the chaos. If the bitch knows what's good for her ass, she will stay as far away from me as possible.

The last thing I wanted my wife to see was me with the bitch, Ava. I don't even know what to say to her. I have never questioned her love for me, but her coming here is confirmation of her love for me. As I head over to the safe house where I had my men take care, I can't help but think about her saying that we had a three-week-old son. I haven't been gone for nine months so she had to have him early. I had so many questions but was too afraid to ask. The look in her eyes was nothing but pure hatred. I can't live knowing that she hates me. Rose' has to understand that everything I did was for us to be able to live comfortably.

"What's up Marco? How is she doing in there?" I asked one of my men, who I had bring her here.

"Mrs. Ramirez is not a happy camper. She's a feisty one, boss. Forgive me if I'm out of line, but I don't think you want to go up there right now." The look on his face let me know that she had given him hell.

"If I want my wife, I have no other choice but to go up there. Try not to laugh if you hear me begging like Keith Sweat." We both laughed and I headed into the crib to holler at Rose'.

I hesitated before placing the key inside the lock. I went inside and Rose' was asleep on the bed. I really missed her beautiful ass. She was sleeping so peacefully that I didn't want to wake her. I undressed, showered and lay in bed with her. I hadn't had a good night's sleep in months. Lying beside Rose' was the best feeling on Earth. I just watched her until I drifted off to sleep.

The next morning I woke up and Rose' was gone. I packed my shit and took flight back to Chicago. I was so fucking mad at her for leaving, but in my heart I knew that I had no right to be mad.

****

Once my plane landed, I headed straight to Madear's house. I knew that's where Rose' would be at. It was early as hell but I didn't care; I needed to talk to Rose'. I knocked on the door several times before Madear opened it.

"Look what the wind done blew in. If I had my shotgun I would shoot you in your ass… got my grandbaby crying and shit. I don't know where you've been and I really don't give a damn. You better get your shit together and make things right with Rose'."

"I'm going to do everything in my power to make it up to Rose'. You know I love my wife, Madear. Where is she?"

"She's at the hospital with the baby, where you need to be."

Madear slammed the door in my face. I couldn't even be mad at her. Madear don't play when it comes to her grandkids. I got in contact with Dino and found out that the baby was at Comer Children's Hospital. After getting the information from the receptionist, I rode the elevator up to the NICU. I never imagined I would be seeing my firstborn son under these conditions. I let out a deep breath before entering the room.

My anxiety level was at an all-time high. It was sad seeing all the babies with tubes coming from everywhere. The nurse led me to my son's incubator and I smiled as I approached him. Rose' wasn't around so I sat in the chair next to his incubator and just stared at him. He was my twin. I placed my hands inside the holes so that I could touch him. His eyes opened up and he stared straight at me.

"You mad at Daddy too, huh? I love you son and I'm sorry for not being here. I'm here now and I'm not going anywhere."

"Don't make promises to him that your black ass can't keep. You need to go ahead on back to Mexico with that bitch Ava. We don't need your ass here. We've been doing fine without you," Rose' said from behind me.

"Don't do that Rose'." I knew she was mad, but all that language and disrespect wasn't even necessary.

"Don't do what, tell the truth? I'm so over this shit with you. Could you please do me and my son a favor? Leave and never come back."

"Excuse me. I think you all should step out. We don't want to make the baby upset. I'll take good care of your son. Go home and get some rest, Mrs. Ramirez. You've been here around the clock," the nurse said as she started checking the baby's vitals.

I took another look at my son and stepped out in the hallway, waiting for Rose' to come out. I knew she was mad at me, but she had me and life fucked up if she thought the shit she said out her mouth was cool.

"Your still here?" Rose' said as she tried to walk past me but I grabbed her.

"Stop with all the fucking disrespect. I know you're mad right now but you need to calm down. Let's go home and talk about this shit Rose'. How the fuck can I make things right if you won't let me?

"In case you didn't get the fucking memo, I don't have a house to go to. Your dead ass mother put me and my daughter out of our home."

"We have a new home. I had it built from the ground up for us. Let's go pick up Heaven and go home. Please give me a chance to explain myself." She reluctantly let me hold her hand and we walked out of the hospital together.

Chapter 28- Rose'

As I rode in the car with Remy, I couldn't even look at him. If I did I would burst into tears. I was all cried out. It was crazy how this man was my husband, my better half, the father of my child but he felt like a stranger to me. I don't know who this man sitting next to me is.

I stared out of the window until we made it to Madear's house. Heaven came running outside full speed ahead. She was so happy to see Remy. I didn't even exist to her once she saw him.

"Heyyy! Daddy I missed you so much. Where have you been?" Heaven asked as she got in the car with us. She hugged Remy's neck from the back and kissed him on his jaw.

"I had to take a vacation baby girl. I missed you too." He hugged and kissed her cheeks. It was good seeing them together. All she does is asks about him; seeing them together warmed my heart.

"Hey Heaven, Mommy don't get no love?"

"Sorry Mommy." She kissed me on the jaw and put her seatbelt on. We continued to drive for another hour. I don't know where the hell we were. There was nothing but roads and trees. When we finally stopped, we came to a huge gate. I watched as Remy used his fingerprint to gain access. The huge gate opened up and we drove up to the front of the house. It was amazing.

The exterior of the home had all white and gold trimmings, all around it. The yard was beautifully manicured. It looked like something out of Home and Garden magazine.

"Welcome home. Do you like it?" Remy asked as we got out of the car.

"I love it, Daddy. I'm so happy you brought us a new house. The mean lady made us leave our other house. Then we had to go live with my Daddy Ace. He hit Mommy and Ms. Diamond all the time."

Leave it to my daughter to run off at the mouth. With the birth of my son and catching Remy in Mexico with Ava, I had put the ordeal with Ace behind me. I kept my eyes glued to the floor because I was too scared to look up. The hairs on the back of my neck were standing up out of the fear of how Remy would look at me.

"Go upstairs and find your room Heaven. I'm sure your daddy made it really beautiful for you."

"What the fuck is she talking about?" Remy said as he walked towards me and pushed me into the wall. Tears fell down my face as I thought about all that I had been through.

"While you were away taking care of business, my daughter and I were being held captive in Ace and Diamond's house. He had me in the basement for like three months. He knew I was pregnant and he still raped me every day. Honey and Neicee found out where I was and when I went to the hospital, I had to give birth to my son at six months.

You have no idea what I've been through since you've been gone. How could you just up and leave us like that? You broke your promise, Remy. You told me everything would be okay and I was safe with you. You lied to me! You lied to me! I hate you so much." I was crying and hitting him all over. I didn't care where the punches landed. I was so fucking mad at him. I hit him until I got tired of swinging. I just fell to the floor and cried. He lifted me up and carried me upstairs to our bedroom.

"I'm so sorry baby. I never meant for any of this to happen. I had to go back to Mexico and off them motherfuckers who crossed my father. If I didn't I wouldn't be standing here with you now. All that shit with Ava was a fucking set-up for me to take back what the fuck they stole from my father. Everything I did was for us. I'm sorry that I wasn't here to protect you and Heaven. Rose', you have to know that I would never put my family in harm's way. I love you, Rose'. Please forgive me for not being here when you needed me." Remy was kissing me all over my face and wiping my tears away.

"I missed you so fucking much," Remy said as he laid me down on the bed. He pulled my shoes off and began tugging at my pants. At first I was hesitant but I had yearned for my husband for months, and finally he was here with me. I needed to feel him, and right now he felt good as fuck. I kissed him on his lips long and hard. He slipped his tongue in my mouth and he tasted so sweet.

Once my pants and panties were off, Remy went straight in for the kill. He was pounding my pussy with so much force I swear I could feel his ass damn near in my chest. I wrapped my legs around his waist and grabbed his ass to bring him in closer to me.

"Please Remy. Don't ever leave me again," I kept saying over and over again. At the same time I was cumming all over him.

"I'll never leave you again baby." As the words left Remy's mouth he came and we both became as one we just laid there and held on to each other. I gently tugged on his dreads. I inhaled deeply and his cologne mixed with the smell of his hair oil had me wet as hell. I felt his dick come back to life inside of me and we went back at it like wild animals. After twenty minutes of doing every position possible, I was stuck. As I lay on Remy's chest, I thought about our marriage and if we were going to make it.

"Thank you Rose'." Remy sat up and stared me directly in the eyes.

"Thank you for what?"

"For giving me my first born son. That shit means the world to me, ma."

I blushed as he kissed me on the lips. I missed this man so much and at this very moment, the only thing that mattered was us and our kids. I had finally found my happy.

Even though there had been hurdles and obstacles standing in our way, I had to forgive Remy for leaving me alone. In my heart I knew he meant well, even if I didn't agree with him fucking the crazy bitch Ava. Remy belonged to me and all I wanted was for us to be happy, have a house full of kids, and grow old together. I deserved happiness and I was going to die getting it.

The next morning we dropped Heaven off to Madear's and went to the hospital. They had been calling me all morning telling me I needed to get there immediately. When we made it to the hospital, the administrator and some police officers were waiting for us. We were escorted into a private area.

"Can somebody please tell us what the fuck is going on with our son?" Remy said as he stood up and knocked the chair over he was sitting in.

"We're sorry to inform you, but your son was kidnapped during the night. We're doing everything possible to find him," the hospital administrator said. I lost all of my senses hearing that my son was gone.

"What the fuck you mean he was kidnapped?" Remy said as he hit the hospital administrator. The police jumped in and he started to fight them and that made them angrier. They tussled and fought with Remy as they tried to put him in handcuffs.

"Please stop fighting, Remy! Please don't arrest him!" I cried and pleaded with the police officers.

"I'm sorry ma'am, but he assaulted a police officer." They finally got the handcuffs on him and escorted him out.

"Don't cry Rose', we're going to find him," he yelled over his shoulder. I laid my head down on the desk and cried harder than I ever have in my life. The very moment I thought I had found my happiness, it was ripped away from me in the blink of an eye. All I could think about was who had my son and why did they kidnap him?

*****

It had been a month since our son had been kidnapped. There had been no clues as to where he was or who could have taken him. I just knew someone was going to call with a ransom demand or some shit, but we got nothing. The person who took our son was a woman but we couldn't see her face clearly on the videotape from the hospital, because she had a hat covering her face. She was dressed in scrubs and had on a badge. That's how she was able to get in and kidnap our son.

With Remy Jr. being gone, there was a strain in my marriage. I couldn't remember the last time I had spent time with Remy. He had been out in the streets along with Boo and Peanut, wreaking havoc trying to find out information about who took our son. Honey and Neicee were also doing what they could do to find him. My father and Madear took Heaven to keep her safe. As for me, I've been sitting around sulking. Not to mention drinking like a damn fish. Pineapple Ciroc had become my best friend, in addition Xanax. It was the only thing that numbed me from all the pain I was experiencing and what I had been through in my life.

Remy didn't want to believe that Ava could have something to do with the disappearance of our son, but I knew this had that bitch name all over it. Only jealous women would do some shit like this. After what Remy did to her, I wouldn't be surprised if she did this crazy shit. Remy felt like Ace had something to do with it but I don't think that. If he wanted to harm the baby, he would have made me have a miscarriage when he was holding me hostage.

To be on the safe side, I was making a trip to the county jail. I didn't tell anybody because I knew they would think I was out of my mind. I actually was out of my mind. My son being gone was taking a toll on me. I was slowly but surely losing my mind.

"What are you doing here Rose'?" Ace said into the phone. I thought he would be looking all rough but he was looking the total opposite. Usually niggas be stressing but he looked like he wasn't worried about shit. That was Ace for you. Crazy motherfucker didn't have a care in the world.

"Did you have something to do with the kidnapping of my son?" Tears were rolling down my face as I sobbed.

"Of course not Rose'. I have no reason to kidnap your son. In case you forgot I've been in here. Plus, I've caused you and my daughter enough pain. I'm sorry for everything I ever did to you. I know it's too late for me to make things right. I plead guilty and I was sentenced to ten years in prison.

I get shipped out tomorrow. I know you view me as a monster and you have every right to think that. I just couldn't deal with the fact that you were with someone else. I hope you find your son safe and unharmed.

Hopefully, when I get out I can build a relationship with my daughter if she doesn't hate me my guts. No matter what, it's my blood running through her veins. Again, I'm sorry for everything. Kiss my daughter for me. Goodbye Rose'."

Ace hung up the phone and walked away. I wasn't expecting that at all. Despite Ace being apologetic, the devil lives inside of him and that would never go away. Ace needs professional help. I hope he gets that while he's away. As far as him building a relationship with Heaven, that will never happen. Remy has officially adopted her and changed her last name to Ramirez.

I believed Ace when he said he had nothing to do with the kidnapping. That only left Ava. That bitch had a motive, and all evidence in my book led to her. When I arrived home there was a package on our doorstep addressed to Remy. As I walked inside the house, the loud smell of Kush invaded my nostrils.

"Hey Husband." I tried to kiss him but he pushed me away from him.

"Where the fuck have you been at?" He drank straight from the Hennessy bottle.

"I had to go out and handle some things." I spoke nervously because Remy was seething with anger.

"So you gone sit and lie in my motherfucking face like I'm some bitch ass nigga? You must've liked for that nigga to hold you hostage and rape your ass. Is that what made you go and see that nigga?" Remy yanked me by the collar of my shirt and slammed me into the wall.

"I only went to see him to ask if he took our son. He doesn't know anything. I needed to talk to him personally, Remy."

"You were supposed to check with me before you decided to go and do some shit like that. I'm handling this shit my own way."

"I'm sorry I didn't tell you Remy. I needed to know. Please find my baby. I'm going to die without him." We stood in the middle of our living room crying our eyes out and holding each other. Remy wasn't the type to cry, but I could tell this shit was hurting him as much as it was hurting me.

"I promise I'm going to find him. Please have faith in your man." Remy kissed me over and over again. After we gathered ourselves, I remembered the package that was addressed to him.

"This came for you." I handed it to him and I watched him open it. It was a DVD with the words "Watch Me" written across it. We both looked at each other before he put inside the DVD player.

I covered my mouth in horror as I watched the same woman who I caught sucking Remy's dick, breastfeeding my son. He had gotten fatter and his hair was long to only be a two month old.

"I'm going to kill this bitch with my bare hands," Remy said as he threw the Hennessy bottle up against the wall.

"I hated this had to happen but you left me no choice, Remy. For years it was always about me and how one day we would settle down. I believed all your fucking promises. It was always you weren't ready to settle down. I was good enough to suck your dick and you fuck me in every one of my holes, but not good enough to be your wife. Let's not forget the numerous abortions I was forced to get because you didn't want any kids.

The first bitch that comes along, you not only move her in your crib that I was never allowed to come to, but you marry the convict ass bitch and have a son with her. He's beautiful by the way. I imagine this is what our son would look like. Do you see what you made me do? I loved you Remy. Why wasn't I good enough? It's okay though; my son loves me if you don't. Ain't that right mommy's little angel." I cried as I watched her stroke his hair and kissed him all over his chunky face.

"Aww! Stop crying little bitch. Go have another baby because this one belongs to me. Say goodbye to him." It was like this bitch was taunting me.

"No, it's goodbye to you bitch!" In an instant, a hooded figure stepped into view and blew her brains out. The person took Remy Jr. out of her arms. He was screaming at the top of his lungs. Me and Remy just looked in shock as the person sat down and started singing to him to calm him down.

"Hush little Baby don't say a word
Momma's going to buy you a mockingbird
And if that mockingbird don't sing
Momma's going to buy you a diamond ring."

The mystery person removed the hood and spoke into the camera. "The both of you will pay dearly for fucking with my heart." I let out a blood curdling scream as I watched in horror as Ava placed a pillow over my son's head and began to smother him.

TO BE CONTINUED

Text SHAN to 22828 to stay up to date with new releases, sneak peeks, contest, and more...

CPSIA information can be obtained at www.ICGtesting.com
Printed in the USA
LVOW04s1511260815

451623LV00021B/957/P